Bill Smith
3413 Logan
Wi-590616
Texas City Texas

Texas City Texas

The Happy Hollisters and the Ice Carnival Mystery

BY JERRY WEST

Illustrated by Helen S. Hamilton

GARDEN CITY, N.Y.

Doubleday & Company, Inc.

LIBRARY OF CONGRESS CATALOG CARD NUMBER 58–9664

PRINTED IN THE UNITED STATES OF AMERICA

Bill Smith
3413 Logan
WI-5-9816
Texas City, Tex

Contents

CHAPTER 1

A WINTER SURPRISE

"OUR snowman's ready for his head!" Ricky Hollister proudly told his brother and sisters.

"Can we finish him before schooltime?" asked Holly.

"Sure," spoke up Pete. He stepped back to admire the huge snowball which formed the snowman's body. The five Happy Hollister children had rolled it in their front yard.

"Oh, it's keen!" said Pam her eyes sparkling with delight. "Come on Sue, baby, let's make the head."

Another fluffy snowball was rolled quickly, and the two boys lifted it into place. But Ricky, on his tiptoes, started to slip backward. To save himself, he flung his arms about the snowman's head.

"Look out!" Pam shrieked. She was too late. Ricky fell to the ground, and the snow head splattered in his face.

"Oh, dear!" Pam said sympathetically. "Are you hurt?"

When Ricky's freckled face grinned through the bits of snow all the children burst out laughing. Nothing bothered red-haired Ricky, who was seven, a year older than pig-tailed Holly. Dark-haired Sue was four, youngest of the Hollisters, and handsome Pete, twelve, the oldest. He had blond hair like Pam, who was eleven.

As Ricky stood up and wiped the snow from his rosy face, Pam said, "Don't worry. We can make our snowman another head."

Just then the front door of the Hollister home opened. A slender, smiling woman stepped out onto the porch. "Time for school!" Mrs. Hollister called.

The children raced up onto the porch where their mother kissed each one good-by and handed them their schoolbooks.

"Hurry!" she urged.

It was Friday and the last day before winter vacation, which added to the children's joy. Now they would have a week to play in the snow, provided the February weather remained cold enough.

The four Hollisters arrived in Lincoln School just as the last bell was ringing. Rosy-cheeked, they kicked off their boots, removed their winter garments, and took seats in their various classrooms. But the thoughts of each child kept wandering back to the half-finished snowman.

When Ricky was asked by his teacher how much

six times six was, he was dreamily looking out the window. Quickly he answered, "A snowman's head," and everyone laughed.

It seemed to the boy as if the hands of the clock crept very slowly toward dismissal time that afternoon. Finally the last bell rang, and the children trooped out of school. Ricky and Holly were among the first to dash along the school sidewalk.

"Come on, let's take the short cut home and finish the snowman!" Ricky urged.

Holly nodded and followed her brother. By cutting cater-cornered across a field they could save time. Both had to step high in the knee-deep snow, and Holly had a difficult time. Once she stopped for a moment to tuck her pigtails into the hood of her snow suit. "Wait for me," she pleaded, and her breath came out in little white puffs.

Ricky took his sister's hand, and together they plodded across the sparkling white field. When they burst into their yard, the two stopped short in amazement.

"Yikes!" Ricky exclaimed. "Our snowman has a head!"

"And arms too!" Holly said, staring unbelievingly.

Not only did the frosty white figure have a head and face but he wore a stocking cap, the peak of which drooped down at a rakish angle nearly touching his carrot nose. The snowman's eyes, made of two

Their snowman seemed to speak!

pieces of coal, sparkled in the afternoon sunshine. For a mouth he had a banana that turned up at the corners.

As Ricky and Holly continued to blink in astonishment their snowman began to speak in a deep, hollow voice. "Hello there!" he said. "I needed a head to think with so I grew one while you were at school."

"He's—he's talking!" Holly cried in awe.

At this moment Pete and Pam raced up, skidding to a halt to stare at the snowman.

The deep voice continued, "Ho, ho! You act as though you'd never seen a talking snowman before. You're the Happy Hollisters, aren't you?"

A weak reply came from Holly: "Y–yes," she stammered.

All at once a grin covered Pete's face. He bent down and whispered in his younger brother's ear.

Ricky grinned too. Then, hunching low, he tiptoed in a wide circle around behind the snowman. "Come out of there, Gramp! We know you!" he called.

Hearing this, the other three dashed to the back of the snowman to see Ricky pulling a chuckling man in storm coat and fur cap from a hiding place scooped out of the big ball.

Grandfather Hollister was lean and rugged. He had a straight nose and a humorous smile. As he hugged his grandchildren he said, "Hope you didn't mind my finishing your snowman and playing a joke on you."

"We loved it," said Pam. "Oh, I'm so glad you came. When did you get here?"

"This morning just after you left for school."

"How long are you staying?" Holly asked.

"For a few days. Gram and I are on our way to Quebec to see the Winter Carnival. Thought we'd come first to see you."

"Where's Gram?" Holly asked, looking around.

As she spoke, Mrs. Hollister, dressed in a heavy coat, stepped onto the porch. She was followed by Sue and a young-looking middle-aged woman with a round face and happy smile.

"Gram! Gram!" the children shouted in unison as they ran toward her. She was nearly knocked over by the enthusiastic hugs and kisses of her grandchildren.

Mr. Hollister's parents, now retired, lived in Froston, Canada, where they owned a group of cottages they rented to winter sportsmen. They had left their place in charge of an assistant so they could take the trip.

"What's Kee-beck?" asked Sue.

"A famous city," said Gramp. "We want to visit it now to see the Mardi Gras."

Gramp and the children took off their boots on the porch and entered the house.

"Tell us more about the Quebec carnival," Ricky begged.

Gramp Hollister sat down in an easy chair. At once Holly and Ricky climbed onto his lap.

"Well," Gramp began, "the carnival has a mascot named *Bonhomme Carnaval*. He's a giant snowman who walks about the streets greeting people."

"A talking snowman!" Pete chuckled. "Is that how you got the idea for our talking snowman?"

"That was it," Gramp admitted, laughing.

"But there's much more to the Quebec carnival," Gram Hollister spoke up. "The parade of floats on the final night is beautiful, and the carnival queen with her duchesses rides through the snowy streets."

"Don't forget the canoe race across the St. Lawrence River," Gramp continued.

This intrigued the girls as well as the boys. When questioned about it, Gramp said that long canoes, manned by five contestants, raced across the ice-filled St. Lawrence from Quebec to Levis on the other side.

"But what if the chunks of ice get in the way?" Ricky asked.

Gramp said that the expert rivermen pulled the canoes up and over the ice into clear water.

"Oh boy, I'd love to see that," Pete remarked.

After the children's mother served hot cocoa and cookies, tom-boy Holly spoke up: "Let's have a snowball war!"

"Okay," Gramp said, and hurried outside with all his grandchildren except Sue.

Gramp took a position behind a tall oak tree with Ricky and Holly at his side. Pete and Pam chose the shelter of a low bush and all began to make light fluffy snowballs as fast as they could. When the two piles had been completed, Ricky cried out, "Ready, aim, fire!"

The air was filled with snowballs whizzing back and forth. A piece of snow went down Holly's neck, but she merely giggled and tossed the ammunition even faster.

At the height of the battle a station wagon came into the driveway directly in the line of fire. "It's Daddy, it's Daddy!" Pam cried out. "Cease fire, everybody!"

At the wheel of the car sat an athletic-looking man with a friendly smile. Mr. Hollister ran *The Trading Post* in Shoreham. It was a combination hardware, toy, and sporting goods shop.

The children's father stopped the car and got out. As he did Pam cried, "Look out, Dad!"

A large hard snowball whizzed through the air and knocked off Mr. Hollister's hat.

"Hey, Ricky!" he cried out. "You shouldn't do that."

"But I didn't!" Ricky protested. He wheeled about toward the street and shouted, "There's the one who did it."

"Joey Brill!" Holly cried.

A fleeting glimpse was enough for the Hollisters to recognize the young bully who had pestered them constantly since they had moved to Shoreham.

"Well, come on, Joey!" Pete called out. "We'll have a snowball fight with you."

But Joey ran away as Mr. Hollister picked up his hat and brushed it off. "I don't mind getting hit with a snowball," he said, "but that one had ice in it." Mr. Hollister put the hat back on his head, grinned, and grasped his father's outstretched hand.

"Hi, Dad!" he said, slapping the older man on the back. "Elaine telephoned me that you were here."

After supper there was more talk about the Quebec carnival. "It's vacation time for us," Pam reminded her parents. "Couldn't we please go see the carnival?"

Mr. and Mrs. Hollister exchanged meaningful glances and smiled but said nothing. Then as Mrs. Hollister served her husband dessert, he whispered something to her.

"It's not polite to have secrets," Holly remarked.

"No, it isn't," her father agreed. "But this is a special secret. I can't tell you now."

"Oh, you're a tease, Daddy," Pam remarked.

Mr. Hollister quickly changed the subject by asking whether Domingo had been given his pail of oats that day. Domingo was the Hollisters' pet burro. He had been sent to them by a rancher out west and lived in a stall in the family's garage.

"Goodness!" Mrs. Hollister said. "I completely forgot about Domingo's supper!"

"I'll take care of him!" Ricky volunteered, and when dinner was over he went to the garage with a bucket of oats. Seeing the food, Domingo stretched his head up and down and said, "Ee aw! Ee aw!"

"Atta boy, Domingo!" Ricky laughed as he set the feed before the hungry animal.

The weather grew colder during the night, and next morning the snow sounded crunchy under foot. The children raced outside with their sleds.

"Let's go over to the long hill and ride down," Pete proposed. "And we'll get Domingo to pull us there."

Tying one sled behind another they formed a train. Then they hitched Domingo to the first one. Pete led the burro for a few paces until all the sleds were under way. Then he hopped onto the first one. Domingo pulled them briskly across the crusty snow toward the nearby hill.

"We're like Eskimos," Holly called as they glided along. "Only we have a burro instead of a dog team."

In a short while Domingo reached the foot of the hill, where dozens of children were sliding down a long grade toward Pine Lake. As Pete halted the donkey one of the sledders suddenly veered from his course and headed straight for the little animal's feet!

CHAPTER 2

TRICKY CANDY

"CAREFUL!" Pete cried out.

He reached forward and grabbed the steering bar of the oncoming sled, inches from the burro's hoofs. It nearly jolted the rider off. Joey Brill!

"Take your hands off!" the boy shouted and leaped up from his sled. Pete let go and also stood up.

Holly's eyes were blazing. "Joey, you tried to hit Domingo on purpose!" she declared hotly. "Just like you hit my daddy yesterday."

"That snowball was meant for Ricky," Joey defended himself with a sneer.

"It had ice in it," Pete said. "You know that's not fair play. Don't do it again, Joey."

"Who's going to stop me?"

"I will!" Pete retorted.

Just then Joey glanced at the ground. He smiled. Then without warning he shoved Pete, who fell backward over his sled and landed with a crash on the hard snow.

Before Pete had time to scramble to his feet, Ricky, his fists flying, pitched headlong into Joey Brill. The bully pushed him to the ground.

Never before had Pam seen Joey act so bravely but she soon learned the reason. Running up behind him was his friend Will Willson.

Now on his feet again, Pete leaped over the sled and lunged at Joey. Grappling, the two boys fell to the snow and rolled over and over.

"Help me, Will!" Joey cried out.

His pal made a move to kick Pete but, before he could do this, Ricky rolled against his legs, sending the older boy sprawling. Before Will had a chance to rise, both Pam and Holly sat on him, while Sue sprinkled snow into his face.

"Hey, let me up!" Will cried out. Then he bellowed, "Joey, these girls are too much for me. Help! Help!"

A knot of children had gathered at the spot, laughing at Will's predicament. Pete, meanwhile, had rolled on top of Joey and pinned his shoulders to the ground.

"Okay! Okay! You win!" Joey said, and Pete let him up.

Ricky and his sisters, meanwhile, caused the crowd to roar with laughter as they grabbed Will's legs and pulled him a short distance in the snow.

"Let go of me! Let go of me!" he begged.

"If you try that again," Ricky said, "we'll make Domingo sit on you!"

The two bullies rose to their feet and brushed themselves off. "You got us this time," Joey said, grumbling. "But I'm going to get even with you."

"Me too," Will threatened. The boys ran off a distance, then turned, and Joey shouted back, "We're going to ruin your snowman!" With that they dashed off, pulling their sleds behind them.

Pam turned to Pete, a look of fear on her face. "We can't let them do that, Pete."

"I'll say not!"

Jumping on their sleds they turned Domingo around and urged him forward. The burro, usually co-operative, decided this would be a good time to rest.

"Please Domingo, hurry, hurry!" Holly begged. But the burro would not move.

"I guess we'll have to unhitch our sleds and run home," Pete said.

After instructing Sue and Holly to remain behind and coax Domingo home, the other three children dashed after Joey and Will. By now the bullies had a good head start and were tiny specks in the distance.

Seeing that they could not all make fast time pulling their sleds, Pete and Pam dropped theirs. "We'll race on ahead, Rick. Bring our sleds," Pam said.

Together the older children dashed toward their

"Please, Domingo, hurry!"

home. Joey and Will, turning around, saw them and ran even faster. In a moment they dashed into the Hollisters' yard. No one was in sight.

"First I'll knock off the head," Joey said.

"And I'll kick the body to pieces," Will bragged as the two boys approached the snowman.

But suddenly a voice made them freeze in their tracks. "Hold it, boys!" boomed a voice with a funny hollow sound.

Startled, Joey backed off, his eyes popping. "Who said that?"

"I did!" came the voice. "Haven't you ever seen a talking snowman before?"

The eyes of the two boys darted this way and that. No one was in sight.

Will managed a half-smile. "There can't really be a talking snowman."

"But there's no one around," Joey argued. "I'm going to get out of here quick!"

The two boys raced out of the yard just as Pete and Pam arrived. "They didn't break our snowman after all!"Pam said bewildered.

The deep voice boomed again, "No, because I stopped them!" With that Gramp Hollister stepped from behind the snowman.

Pete and Pam bent over, howling with laughter. And when the other children joined them with Domingo a few minutes later they giggled to think Joey and Will had been so neatly fooled.

Domingo, seeing everyone laughing, bobbed his head and said, "Ee aw! Ee aw!"

Gramp explained that he had walked out into the yard and was behind the snowman just as the bullies arrived. Hearing their threats, he had started to talk.

Now Gramp joined the children and together they returned to the hill. With no one to bother them they had a lot of fun sledding all morning. After lunch they played in the snow. As the fading daylight silhouetted the trees they all went indoors, their faces tingling from the bracing air.

When supper ended Pete said, "Dad, what's this big mystery you were talking about?"

"Tell us, please," Ricky urged.

"All right," Mr. Hollister said finally. "And Elaine, get your coat and hat. We mustn't be late for the meeting we promised to attend."

As the children clustered around Mr. Hollister's chair, he smiled and said, "This is a mystery about a *cariole*."

"What's that?" Pam asked.

Her father explained that a *cariole* was a French-Canadian sleigh. He had ordered one as a Christmas gift for his children. Domingo was to pull it.

"But Christmas was a long time ago," Sue remarked, "and Santa Claus didn't bring it."

"No, that's the mystery," Mr. Hollister went on as the children listened openmouthed. "I wrote a letter to the sleigh maker but I haven't heard from him."

"Did you pay for the sleigh, Dad?" Pam asked.

Her father nodded. "It isn't so much the money," he said, "but the *cariole* is beautiful, and I wanted you children to have it."

"Where was the *cariole* to be made?" said Pete.

"In Quebec," Mr. Hollister continued, "and——"

Mrs. Hollister walked in, ready to leave. Her husband glanced at his watch. "I'll tell you children more about the mystery later," he said.

The children looked so disappointed that Gram proposed they have a taffy pull.

"Oh goody," said Sue and Holly added, "Isn't it wonderful to have a grandma who knows all about taffy?"

Hearing this, Mr. Hollister laughed. "She sure does. Gram got me unstuck plenty of times when I was a little boy."

As the front door closed behind Mr. and Mrs. Hollister, the children followed Gram into the kitchen. Pam brought out a large kettle and under Gram's direction soon had brown sugar, butter, and water bubbling on the stove.

"Is it ready? Is it ready?" cried little Sue, jumping up and down excitedly.

"Just a minute now," Gram said, dipping a spoon into the seething mass. She dropped a bit of syrup into a cup of cold water to test it. Holding the piece between her fingers, Gram said it was just hard enough to be worked. She put in some vanilla and stirred the taffy.

"Pete," Gram directed, "get some butter for our hands."

"Why do we put butter on our hands?" Holly asked in surprise.

"To keep the taffy from sticking," came the reply. "And also, you won't burn your hands."

At this moment Gram announced that the syrup was ready. The children all hurriedly rubbed their hands with butter and stood in line by the stove. When the syrup had cooled and thickened a little Gram carefully ladled a small amount into each of the outstretched hands.

"Now hurry," she said. "Toss it from hand to hand until you can hold it in your fingers. Then pull it quickly before it gets too hard."

"Yikes!" Ricky said. "This is fun."

"And a little hot too," Holly said, raising her eyebrows.

Five pairs of hands worked eagerly, pulling the taffy one way then the other. All this time the family's pet collie, Zip, had been lying in a corner watching the scene. Ricky turned to him.

"Watch me, Zip, old boy. I'll go faster than any of the others!"

Swish, swish, swish. He pulled the taffy with all his might. But in his enthusiasm Ricky dropped the candy. *Plop!* It landed on the floor.

At once Zip jumped forward and quickly snatched the sticky mass in his mouth. Then he began to wave his head from side to side, letting out little growls.

"Oh!" Pam said. "The taffy's stuck on Zip's teeth! He can't get it off!"

"Here, boy," Pete called. "I'll get it off for you."

Now everybody was laughing at poor Zip. The dog raised his lips, looking very funny as he tried to pull the taffy from his teeth with his forepaws.

Pete laid his own taffy on a plate and, stooping down, carefully pulled as much of the sticky stuff from Zip's teeth as he could. Then he put a bowl of warm water on the floor.

"Here, Zip," he said encouragingly, "drink that. It will wash the taffy off your teeth." The dog lapped up the water gratefully.

While Pete had been helping Zip, Ricky had picked up his brother's taffy and pulled it. Gram and Gramp helped Holly and Sue. Finally they were able to juggle the sticky mass from hand to hand, then pull it out into long ribbons, doubling it over and pulling it out again.

"This is lots of fun." Sue giggled, her eyes shining with excitement.

She held the candy mass high above her head. Just then the loop of taffy dropped. Some if it caught in her hair. The rest fell down like a necklace.

"Oh, help!" Sue cried out when she found the taffy refused to budge.

CHAPTER 3

THE FIRST CLUE

"GRAM! Help! I'm all gooey with taffy!" Sue cried out as she tried in vain to remove the sticky candy from her neck and hair.

"Ha, ha!" Ricky laughed, "Sue's wearing a snake."

Pam giggled. "A taffy snake! Look out he doesn't bite you with his sweet tooth."

Gram went to Sue's aid. After moistening her fingers with warm water she uncoiled the taffy from the little girl's neck. Then she washed the rest off Sue's hair with a wet cloth.

"I want a clean piece," Sue pleaded and Pam gave her a section of her strand.

Now Gram showed the children how to roll the long pieces of taffy between the palms of their hands. Then the rolls were stretched out on a floured cutting board and sliced into bite-sized pieces. After that they were placed on a tray and covered with a sheet of waxed paper.

Ricky popped two of the candies into his mouth. "Um, yum!" he said.

The others helped themselves and presently Holly said, "Now I know how Zip felt. It's all stuck to my teeth!"

The utensils were washed and put back in their proper places by the time Mr. and Mrs. Hollister returned. The children gave them pieces of the taffy, which they declared was the best they had ever tasted.

Seated in the living room once more, Ricky said, "Dad, will you tell us more about your mystery?"

Mr. Hollister smiled. "I haven't told you the most important part."

"Oh, what is it?" they cried in unison.

"I would like——" Mr. Hollister paused. "I would like my young detectives to find the *cariole* for me."

"What!"

"You mean it?"

"Oh, Daddy, you're a dream!"

Mr. Hollister was deluged with enthusiastic hugs and grins from his daughters and sons.

"That means we're going to Quebec!" Pete declared. "Yippee!"

"There's only one hitch," Mr. Hollister said, stroking his chin and making a wry face. "I can't leave my business for too long."

"You don't have to!" Pam remarked. "Why can't Gram and Gramp take us detectives to Quebec? Then you and Mother come up next weekend to get us!"

"Not a bad idea," her father replied. "What do you think of that, Elaine?"

In answer Mrs. Hollister glanced at Gram and Gramp. "It will be up to you two," she declared, smiling. "Do you think you can manage it?"

"Of course we can," Gram said without hesitation. "Our sedan will hold all the children. We can stay at the Hotel Forteresse, overlooking the St. Lawrence River."

"Yikes!" Ricky exclaimed. He grabbed Holly's hands, and together they danced about wildly.

Pam's face flushed with excitement. She had always wanted to see the historic Canadian city which had been settled by the French many years before.

"Quebec was the scene of a great battle, wasn't it?" she asked.

"A snowball fight?" Ricky put in.

"Something much more tragic," Gramp replied, and told of the battle which took place between the defending French and the attacking British.

"The generals," Gramp continued, "were James Wolfe for the British and Louis Joseph de Montcalm for the French."

"Tell us more about it, please!" Holly begged.

"Under cover of darkness," Gramp related, "Wolfe landed with 1600 men in a cove a mile and a half along the St. Lawrence River west of the city. Reinforcements swelled his ranks to 3600."

"Didn't the French know about it?" Pete asked.

Gramp said that the defenders were caught by surprise. The British, climbing the steep cliff, gained the heights of the Plains of Abraham, where they drew up in battle formation. The gallant French attacked, but the British won.

"And," Gram spoke up with a sad sigh, "both Wolfe and Montcalm fell, mortally wounded."

Pam looked sad. "I'm glad the French and the British don't fight any more," she said, "because they're both such nice people."

"Indeed they are," Gramp Hollister remarked. "And when we go to Quebec you'll see the descendants of those gallant Frenchmen."

Gramp Hollister then went on to tell the children that it had taken a lifetime to build the great wall around the old city and only two hours to lose the battle defending it!

"We can see lots of old things while we're in Quebec," said Pam. "Oh, won't it be exciting?"

"And it'll be fun to enjoy the winter sports," Pete added.

"Don't forget you have a detective job to do," Mr. Hollister warned. "I'll give you children a couple of clues to start you off."

He went to the desk in the corner of the living room. Reaching into a drawer, he pulled out a snapshot of a sleigh.

"This is a *cariole*," he said. "The same kind that was to be built for us. The sleigh maker's name is Victor Tremblay. He was to paint the initials "H.H." in scroll letters on the front of our *cariole*."

"H.H. for Happy Hollisters!" Pete exclaimed. "Dad, we should be able to find the sleigh if we look hard enough."

"But maybe the *cariole* was never built," Pam ventured.

"In that case find Victor Tremblay and ask him why," said Mr. Hollister.

"When may we go?" Holly cried excitedly.

"How about day after tomorrow?" Gramp suggested. "Then we'll get to Quebec in plenty of time to see the last few days of the Mardi Gras."

"Fine," said Mrs. Hollister. "The children's father and I will arrive next weekend to bring them home."

Pam quickly made a note of Victor Tremblay's address in Quebec, adding, "Strange your letters never reached him, Dad."

"Maybe they did," Pete spoke up, "and the fellow never bothered to write back."

Mr. Hollister was inclined to think that the sleigh maker had not received the letters.

"I think Dad's right," said Mrs. Hollister. "Something may have happened to the man before they reached him."

"But wouldn't the letters have been returned to us?" Pete asked.

"Not if someone is holding them for him."

"Well, we'll soon find out," Pete declared hopefully.

When Holly and Sue went upstairs at eight o'clock, Holly climbed into her pajamas, then went to sit cross-legged on her little sister's bed.

"Let's play a game," she proposed.

"What kind?" Sue asked.

"I know!" Holly said impishly. "Let's play the battle of Quebec. The rug can be a make-believe river, and the cliff——" She looked about. Her eyes finally lighted on the headboard of Sue's old-fashioned bed. "This can be the cliff!" she said, pointing.

Hopping down, she pulled the headboard away from the wall. Sue, in a frilly blue nightgown with yellow polka dots, jumped on the bed. "I'll be the calm general," she said, "and you can be the bad wolf, Holly."

This made the older girl chuckle. "Oh, silly," Holly said, "he wasn't really a wolf. But if you want to be General Montcalm, all right."

Holly stood behind the headboard. "Now, when I climb over the cliff," she said, "you try to stop me."

Crash! Holly fell backward.

Sue picked up a pillow. "This'll be my cannon," she said.

"Ha, ha, a pillow cannon. That won't hurt me!" Holly said as she started to climb up over the headboard.

Sue lifted the pillow over her head with both hands, to be ready. She let it go. The pillow hit her sister in the face just as she was teetering over the top.

Crash!

With a little cry Holly fell backward and landed on the floor with a bang that jarred the house. Sue Hollister was frightened by her sudden victory. Tears gathered in her eyes as she leaned over the headboard to see Holly sprawled on the floor. "Oh dear, are you hurted?" she asked.

Holly rose slowly, pressing her hand to the back of her head.

Mrs. Hollister burst into the room. "Goodness!" she cried. "What happened?"

"A pillow cannon ball hit me," Holly said, trying to keep back the tears. "Feel here."

Her mother put a hand to the back of Holly's head. A bump was rising rapidly.

"Pam," Mrs. Hollister called, "bring me some ice cubes and a towel."

When Pam carried them in Mrs. Hollister wrapped the cubes in the towel and pressed them against Holly's bump. Her head soon felt better.

"I didn't mean to hit her so hard," Sue said contritely.

"Oh, that's all right," Holly said.

She insisted that Gram and Gramp both feel her "Battle of Quebec" bump before she went to bed. Gramp chuckled. "It isn't always the boys who get into trouble with their high jinks, is it?" he said as he turned off the light in Holly's room.

At breakfast next morning Gram said the children must learn to speak a few words of French. "We'll have a lesson right now."

Before it started Ricky peered out the window to see that the snowman was still intact, then the children became quiet.

"Everybody in Quebec speaks French," Gram said, adding that many children there knew very little English. "What is the first word you would like to learn?"

Pam spoke. "Please."

Gram answered, "*S'il vous plaît.*"

The children repeated, "*S'il vous plaît.*"

Holly chuckled. "It sounds like 'See you play.' "

The others repeated the expression many times until even little Sue seemed to know it well.

The next word was *merci,* or thank you. Then came *bon jour,* or good morning.

"I'm hungry," said Ricky.

"That's *j'ai faim*," Gram Hollister said.

"Oh no, I'm really hungry," Ricky declared.

"You just finished breakfast, silly," Pam reminded him.

But Ricky said *j'ai faim* so well that the others excused him to eat an extra piece of bread and jam. Soon the lesson was over, and all the children went outside to play. Holly and Sue had fun making the snowman talk when people passed by. Pam hitched Domingo to the cart and went shopping for her mother. The boys were invited to go ice boating on Pine Lake with Dave Mead, one of Pete's friends.

The day sped by quickly. At suppertime Mrs. Hollister announced that all the suitcases were packed for the trip. "Supper is almost ready," she said. "Children, wash your hands. And, Pete, did you feed Domingo?"

Pete gasped. He had been so busy reading in the encyclopedia how the British stormed the gates of old French Quebec that he had forgotten all about the burro.

Putting on his boots and jacket, Pete hurried outside. A few minutes later he burst back into the kitchen.

"What's the matter?" Pam asked, seeing a frightened look on her brother's face.

"Domingo—Domingo's gone!" Pete replied wildly.

CHAPTER 4

A SPOOKY NIGHT

ALONG with their parents, Pete and Pam raced to the garage. The doors stood open, and Domingo was nowhere to be seen.

"Look! His rope was untied," Pam said, pointing.

"Here are his hoofprints!" Pete added. The moonlight shining on the snow clearly showed the path that the burro had taken. Intermingled with the animal's tracks were two sets of boot marks.

"Oh!" Pam exclaimed as she followed the prints down the driveway to the street. "I'll bet Joey and Will did this to get even with us."

Pete and Pam followed the tracks along the street a short distance, but the prints became lost in a maze of tracks at the first intersection.

"No use to go any farther," Pete said downcast. "Domingo might have gone in any direction from here."

Tears came to Pam's eyes as she returned to the

house. "We may never see Domingo again," she said fearfully.

Mr. and Mrs. Hollister were as sad as their children about the missing pet.

"Let's telephone police headquarters and tell Officer Cal Newberry," Pete suggested. (The friendly policeman had often helped the children solve mysteries.)

But a call to headquarters revealed that Cal had left for the day. Pete told the desk sergeant of Domingo's disappearance.

"We'll look for your burro immediately," came the reply, "and I'll tell Cal about it the minute he reports back."

The Hollister children went to bed with heavy hearts and a secret prayer that their pet would be returned safely and quickly. Before breakfast the next morning Officer Cal phoned Pete, who answered, listened eagerly, thanked the policeman, and reported the conversation to his family. Joey and Will had been questioned but both had alibis. They had not left their homes the night before.

"Cal says he will keep hunting for Domingo," Pete added. "We should enjoy our trip and not worry."

Holly cocked her head. "If Officer Cal is looking for Domingo, he'll find him," she said confidently.

Shortly after church services the suitcases were packed into Gram and Gramp Hollister's sedan. Pam climbed in front with Gram and Gramp while the other children sat comfortably in the back seat of the roomy car.

"Good-by and good luck!" their parents called. "See you soon."

As Grandfather Hollister drove along, the sky became overcast, and shortly after they had stopped for lunch it began to snow. The windshield wipers worked furiously as the heavy, wet snow piled onto the car.

"I think we'd better telephone ahead for motel reservations," Gramp said finally as he pulled into a service station.

While the tank was being filled he made the call, then they set off again. But travel was slow. The snow fell faster and grew deeper.

"I hope we get there soon." Pam worried as the driving became more hazardous.

All the while Sue had been very quiet. "Don't be frightened, dear," Gram said, turning to smile at the little girl.

"Oh, I'm not," Sue replied cheerily. "I'm just thinking."

"About what?"

"Birdies."

This reply made everyone chuckle. "What about the birdies?" Pam queried.

Sue put a chilly finger to her cheek and said dreamily, "When birdies go to bed, do they take off their wings?" Everyone broke into laughter at this remark.

Gramp had hardly finished chuckling when suddenly in the gathering dusk he saw a dog lope across the road in front of him. Quickly he applied his brakes. The sedan swerved. It teetered at a dangerous angle, then slipped into a ditch by the side of the road! The car came to a stop with a dull thud, throwing its passengers against one another.

"Oh dear! What'll we do now?" Pam cried.

"Everybody stay calm," Gramp said in a reassuring voice. "We'll wait here until a car comes by to help us."

"But they'll never see us down here," Holly wailed.

"I'll turn on my lights and honk to attract their attention."

The Hollisters sat quietly for a few minutes, watching the darkness sift down from the sky along with the driving snow. Then, looming out of the distance, came two headlights.

"Now we'll get out," said Holly hopefully.

But, to the travelers' dismay, neither their lights nor horn responded when Gramp tried them, and before the snowbound group knew it the truck had passed them.

"Maybe something happened to your battery, Gramp," Pete suggested.

He and Ricky offered to walk and find help. Gram,

however, thought they had better remain in the car. "I wouldn't want any of you to get lost at night in this terrible storm," she said.

The motor was kept running in order to provide heat in the sedan, and the windows left open a crack for ventilation. The wind howled. Snow drifted and banked up against the windows. Finally the Hollisters had no view of the outside.

"I hear something coming!" cried Pam.

"It sounds like a snowplow!" Gramp said.

"Hurray! We're rescued!" Ricky shouted.

But the boy spoke too soon. When Gramp tried to open the door to signal the man, it would not budge. By the time he forced it open, the plow was way beyond. The driver, apparently thinking that the car was abandoned, had not stopped. Instead, the plow had piled more snow on the marooned sedan! Gramp's shouts were lost in the wind.

"Well," he said, closing the door again, "we may have to stay in the car all night."

"Yikes! This is a real adventure!" Ricky exclaimed.

Soon Sue fell asleep, and Holly did also shortly afterwards. But they were both awakened when Pete suddenly cried out, "Crickets! Look at this!"

He pointed to the window at his side. Two holes the size of quarters were being melted in the snow clinging to the window glass.

"It's positively spooky!" said Pam.

"The horse found us!"

Gram and Gramp were mystified. "I'll have to get out and see what's causing this," Gramp said.

Pushing and hauling on the door, he finally opened it and stepped out into the blizzard.

"What is it?" Gram called.

"Believe it or not," came Gramp's startled voice, "there's a horse here! The poor fellow's lost. He was breathing on the window!"

Hardly had Gramp said this when a light appeared not far from the sedan.

"Hello there!" Gramp called out.

"Hello!" was the reply. "I'm looking for my horse."

"He's right here!" cried Pam, who had wriggled out and was standing beside her grandfather.

Soon a man appeared carrying a lantern. He wore a heavy jacket and a fur hat.

"I'm George Moulin," the stranger said. "I have a farm down the road. Brownie, my horse, here, was frightened by dogs and ran away. I'm glad you found him."

"We didn't find him," Holly chirped. "He found us!"

"And thank goodness too," Gram remarked. "Otherwise we might have stayed here all night without being found."

The farmer said with a smile, "Come, follow me. I'll take you to my farm for the night."

The Hollisters took their small bags from the trunk of the car, and Pete put Sue on his shoulders. Everyone clambered up the embankment. Then, with Farmer Moulin leading the way with his horse, they followed single file through the deep snow. Gramp held Holly by the hand and pulled her along through the deeper drifts.

Arriving at the farmer's house, the Hollisters stamped the snow from their feet and entered the kitchen. How warm and cozy it was, heated by an old-fashioned coal range!

"Come meet our visitors!" the farmer called to his wife in the next room.

Mrs. Moulin, a sturdy-looking woman with black hair and a lean firm face, was surprised to see her snowbound guests. "Oh, you poor things," she cried out as she led the children to the stove and helped them take off their wet coats.

"Thank you very much," the young visitors chorused.

Gramp telephoned the motel, advising the manager of their plight and canceling the reservations.

After coats had been hung up to dry, the farmer's wife prepared a hot supper. During the meal the children chattered about their adventure.

"You'll enjoy Quebec," Mr. Moulin said. "My mother and father migrated from there to the United States, but always went back to see the Mardi Gras."

When they finished the steaming hot homemade stew, apple sauce, and chocolate cake, the weary travelers were ready for bed. It seemed to Pam that no sooner had her head touched the down pillow than it was morning again.

"Well now," said the farmer after they had eaten a breakfast of scrambled eggs and homemade sausage, "we'll hitch Brownie to our sleigh and return to your car. I'm sure we can pull it out of the ditch."

The children ran for their coats and boots. Pete found his grandmother's and helped her put them on.

After thanking Mrs. Moulin for her generous hospitality, the Hollisters followed the farmer to the barn. Pete helped Mr. Moulin slide back the big doors.

The sight that greeted their eyes made Pam cry out in wonderment. "A *cariole* just like the one we ordered!" she exclaimed.

The farmer was surprised. "How did you know this was a *cariole?*" he asked.

Bubbling over with excitement, the children quickly told the story of the sleigh which was never delivered to them in Shoreham.

"And we're going to try to locate Victor Tremblay when we get to Quebec and find out why," Pete concluded.

Mr. Moulin's eyes widened. "Tremblay!" he said. "He's the man who made this *cariole!*"

"Really?" Gram asked in amazement.

"Tell us about it," Pam urged.

As the farmer walked to Brownie's stall and hitched him to the sleigh, he told the Hollisters that a man named Pierre Tremblay once had worked for him. Pierre had a cousin named Victor, a sleigh maker. It was from Victor that Mr. Moulin had bought this *cariole*.

Brownie pulled the sleigh from the barn. Plumes of steam issued from his nostrils into the frosty morning air.

"Maybe you can tell us where Victor Tremblay has gone," Pam said as Gram, Gramp, and Sue climbed into the sleigh, and the bags were put in.

The farmer shook his head sadly. "I wish I could help you," he said, "but the only thing I know is that Victor Tremblay's family comes from an island in the St. Lawrence River."

"Oh boy!" Ricky said. "That's a long, long river."

"Indeed it is."

As Brownie moved off the children followed. When they arrived at the half-buried car, Mr. Moulin unhitched Brownie, leaving the whiffletree attached to the traces. Then he tied a rope from the whiffletree to the car bumper.

"Giddap! Giddap!" he cried, and Brownie strained against the taut rope.

The car moved a few inches, then a few feet.

"Hurray!" Ricky cried out.

Gramp Hollister grinned, but his smile suddenly turned into a frown. *Snap!* The rope parted, and the car slid back into the ditch.

CHAPTER 5

BONHOMME CARNAVAL

"WE'LL never get to Quebec!" Ricky groaned.

"Oh yes, we will!" his brother called out.

He ran into the center of the road to flag an oncoming truck. The driver stopped and jumped down from the cab.

"In trouble, eh?" he said. "I have just what you need to pull your car out of the ditch!" he added smiling.

Walking around to the back of the truck he pulled out a stout chain. With Pete's help he quickly attached it to the Hollister car. Then, jumping back behind the wheel of the truck, the helpful driver started his vehicle slowly forward.

"It's coming!" Pam declared joyfully as the sedan moved out of the ditch inch by inch.

Finally the car was on the road again.

"You're a nice man," said Sue as the driver stepped down to unfasten the chain.

"Glad to help," he said. "Anything else I can do?"

"Can you wait until I see if the motor will start?" Gramp asked.

He now tested the starter, lights, and horn. None would work. In a jiffy the truck driver had the hood up. After glancing at the machinery he took some tools from the truck, tinkered a few minutes, then said:

"Try her now."

Gramp used the starter. *Whrrr!* It worked, and the motor roared.

"That was neat," Pete said. "What did you do?"

The truck driver laughed as he put down the hood. "Used a little magic. That's all." He jumped into his truck and hurried off.

"Well, Mr. Moulin," Gramp said, "I guess we're on our way again. Thank you very much for being so kind to us."

The farmer smiled and offered his hand to the Hollisters. "I hope you solve your mystery of the *cariole*," he said, "and if I hear any news about it I'll let you know."

With a crunchy sound of tires on the hard snow the family drove along as fast as safety would permit.

"I had hoped to reach Quebec by late afternoon," Gramp said when they stopped for lunch. "But it looks now as if it'll be dark by the time we get there."

"That should be fun," Gram spoke up. "Quebec is very beautiful at night."

Darkness had already settled by the time they reached Canada. A little later they crossed the long bridge spanning the St. Lawrence River.

"Look!" Pam called out. "There's Quebec."

The distant lights twinkled along a bluff rimming the ice-filled river.

"It's just like a fairy necklace," said Holly with a sigh. "Hurry, Gramp, I want to see more of it."

They rode along a broad, straight road leading to the old city. Then they turned right on a narrow street and were immediately stopped by a procession of cars halted in front of them.

"Crickets! What's happened?" said Pete, craning his neck for a better look.

"There's a fire up ahead," Ricky said. "Let's get out and look."

"That's not a fire!" Holly objected. "People are carrying torches."

Suddenly the sound of music, accompanied by children's voices, came to their ears.

"What are they singing, Gram?" Sue asked.

"The carnival song, dear."

The words were in French, but the Hollisters could

make out the merry words, *Carnaval, Mardi Gras, Carnaval.*

Since all the children were eager to watch the parade, Gramp found a place to park. They all got out and hurried to the cross street where the gay festivities were under way.

"Yikes! I've never seen a parade in the snow before!" Ricky exclaimed.

A band went by, illuminated by youngsters holding torches. Immediately behind them came a float which caused the Hollisters to gasp in amazement.

"A snowman! A giant snowman!" exclaimed Sue as she jumped up and down.

"He's ten times larger than ours!" Ricky said.

They all gazed up at the towering figure.

"He looks so gay!" Pam said admiringly.

"That's *Bonhomme Carnaval,*" Gramp told the children.

The jolly snowman wore a sash tied high around his ample middle. On his head was a jaunty hat. A big smile spread over his papier-mâché face as his eyes blinked off and on. Crowds of young people trooped behind *Bonhomme Carnaval,* shouting and singing.

"Let's join them," Pete suggested eagerly.

At a nod from Gram the Hollisters followed the revelers along the street. It led into a large square, in the center of which was a palace made of huge

"A giant snowman!"

blocks of ice. Spotlights hanging from nearby trees made it shimmer and glow in the frosty night.

"Another *Bonhomme Carnaval!*" Pam said gleefully as they drew closer.

"And this one's carved out of ice!" Pete chuckled.

Now the paraders turned their attention from the floats to the gigantic figure seated on a throne against the side of the ice palace.

"He's a trillion times bigger than our snowman!" Ricky said, goggle-eyed.

"Oh, I'm so happy we came to Quebec!" Pam remarked, taking in the beautiful scene.

As the Quebec children pressed closer to the giant *Bonhomme Carnaval* their flickering torches cast shadows over the smiling ice face. The French-Canadian children babbled excitedly in their native tongue.

Flashlight bulbs began to pop as photographers took pictures of the festivities. One of them called out in English, "We need two kids for his lap."

Another photographer nearby called back, "Take your pick. We have hundreds of them here."

"How about using visitors?" called the first photographer. "It'll make better publicity." With that his eyes lighted on the Hollisters. From their traveling clothes he knew they were not natives of Quebec.

"Do you want to help me?" the man said, smiling at Ricky and Holly.

"Yes!" Ricky said eagerly, pushing forward through the crowd and pulling Holly by the hand. Reaching the photographer, Ricky added, "What would you like us to do?"

"Sit on *Bonhomme Carnaval's* lap while we take your picture."

"Way up there?" Holly asked, pointing.

The photographer smiled and nodded.

"But how do we get up there?" Ricky wanted to know, and Gram asked the photographer if it would be safe climbing up.

The man laughed. "I have a ladder just for this purpose. Here it comes."

A tall policeman wearing a heavy blue coat and a fur cap pressed through the crowd carrying the ladder. He placed it against the front of *Bonhomme Carnaval*. Holly scrambled up first, followed by Ricky, as the crowd cheered. Each child sat down on a giant knee of the ice figure.

"Isn't this fun?" Pam said, looking up at her brother and sister. But as more flashlights brightened the scene like winking stars Pam suddenly grasped her brother's arm. "Look!" she cried out. "Holly's slipping!"

Since the ladder had been removed when the picture taking started, Holly had nothing to hold onto. Inch by inch she slipped down over the smooth knee of the ice giant.

A look of consternation came over her face. "Help! Help!" she called.

Ricky reached for his sister but was too far away to catch her. The crowd below gasped as the little girl slipped off *Bonhomme Carnaval's* knee.

"Oh!" Pam screamed.

Down Holly plunged—right into the arms of the tall policeman with the fur cap! At first a gasp went up from the onlookers, then a cheer when they realized that Holly had not been hurt.

"*Merci, merci,*" she said as the policeman set her safely on the snowy pavement.

"Oh, officer," Ricky called down from his perch, "may I do the same thing?"

At first the French-speaking policeman did not understand. When the photographer explained, he looked up and grinned at the boy. "*Sautez, mon petit garçon,*" he called, and stood with outstretched arms.

Impishly Ricky skidded off the other knee and jumped down into the policeman's grasp.

"Say, these are great pictures!" said a photographer who had snapped both sliding scenes.

After Ricky and Holly had given the photographer their names, the Hollisters returned to the car and drove toward their hotel.

"Why, we're going to live in a castle!" Pam declared as they neared the towering structure.

The hotel stood on the edge of the cliff overlooking

a cluster of old houses far beneath on the river front. As they pulled up to the door one attendant took their baggage while another parked their car across the street.

Inside was a large lobby. People lounged about or stood talking in groups. Some wore lovely evening clothes while others were attired in ski togs.

After Gramp Hollister registered for the family they took an elevator to the fifth floor. The bellboy ushered them into a suite of rooms overlooking the river.

Ricky raced to the window and looked down. "Gram," he called out, "what's that long white thing down there?"

"Oh, you must mean the toboggan run," Gram Hollister answered, following him to the window.

"May we have a ride on it?"

"Tomorrow. But now you all must get ready for bed," she said.

The suitcases were hastily unpacked.

"Where's mine with my pajamas?" Holly said, glancing about.

After a search it was decided that the suitcase must have been left in the car.

"Pete and I will go down and get it for you," Pam volunteered.

Slipping into their coats again, the two children went down to the lobby, then stepped outside into the cold windy night. They were just about to cross the street to their car when suddenly a roaring, crackling sound startled them. Pam looked frightened.

Pete glanced upward, then in alarm shouted, "Look out, Pam! Duck!"

Grabbing his sister, Pete pushed her to the wall of the building.

CHAPTER 6

COLLISION!

THERE was a grinding, crashing sound as something hit the sidewalk a few feet from Pete and Pam. The children shielded their faces as a sheet of ice shattered to bits.

"Oh, Pete!" Pam said with a shiver, "we might have been killed! Where did that come from?"

Her brother looked up at the tall building and noted that the roof was steeply sloped and covered with copper.

Just then the doorman stepped out. Seeing what had happened, he explained that the weight of the ice caused it to slide off the roof. "You can hear it coming," he said, "so you'd have plenty of time to get out of the way."

Pete grinned ruefully. "I'm glad you told us," he said. "Next time we hear a sound like that we'll run!"

Still shaking from their fright, the children hurried across the street and found Holly's missing suitcase in the car.

"I'm glad it's here and not back at the Moulins'," said Pete.

The next morning, after breakfast in the hotel's ornate dining room, Pete declared that he was eager to start sleuthing for the missing *cariole*.

"I know you're impatient to solve the mystery," Gram said. "But we can't start just yet. Suppose you children wait outside on the terrace for Gramp and me. We have a few letters to write."

"We'll hurry," Gramp promised. "Pete, will you and Pam take care of the younger ones?"

The older Hollister children promised they would, and Gram and Gramp stepped into the elevator. The five Happy Hollisters walked out of the hotel onto a broad terrace atop the walled bluff overlooking the river.

"Oh, see that big boat!" Ricky said, pointing to a large, double-decked craft starting across the river from the opposite shore.

"It must be a ferryboat," Pete remarked. As it came closer the children could see that the boat carried both people and automobiles.

"Yikes! It's going to hit an ice floe!" Ricky said.

Sue put her hands to her ears as if to shut out the noise of a crash. But the ferryboat plowed right into the ice floe, shuddered a moment, and continued across the river.

"Crickets! They're pretty strong boats," Pete remarked.

"I'd like to ride on one," said Holly.

The five children now turned their attention to the toboggan slide which stretched along the terrace and up a steep slope.

"Here comes a toboggan now!" Pete cried out. "Look!"

Three riders zipped down the icy slope, flashed along the grooved course, and finally came to a stop near where the Hollisters were standing.

"That's keen!" Ricky said. All the children wanted to ride on it but knew they must be patient.

While Pam and Pete stood fascinated by the speeding toboggans, Sue noticed something else that looked interesting. It was a shed at the top of a long sloping shaft which led from the summit of the cliff to a cluster of houses far below. Taking Holly and Ricky by the hand, she pulled them toward it. People were coming out of the shaft and others were going in.

"What is that?" Ricky asked a policeman standing nearby.

"*Ascenseur*," he said.

"A what?" Ricky asked.

The policeman smiled. "An elevator. It takes people up and down between the upper and lower towns."

"May we ride it?" Holly asked.

"Of course, if you have the fare."

Ricky reached into his pocket and pulled out a few coins. "Is this enough?"

When the policeman nodded, the three children opened the door and walked into the shed. After paying their fare they watched the elevator coming up. It was a large, box-like contraption which was hauled up and down the slope on stout cables.

Another door opened, and they walked inside. Then with a grinding noise the elevator descended the slope and stopped at the base of the cliff. The door opened, and the children stepped out.

Now they could look up and get a view of the great wall with the hotel perched at the top.

"This is fun!" Ricky said as they walked down a narrow street. The sign said *Petit Champlain*.

Holly chuckled. "What a funny street!" she said. "It has steps on it."

Glancing to his left, the boy saw that the street suddenly became a long series of steps going up to the next block. In the center was a shiny iron hand-railing which glistened in the sun. The Hollisters realized at once why the railing shone so brightly. It was kept polished by many small children who were sliding gleefully down it on their way to school.

Seeing the curious Hollisters, one of the boys said, "*Regardez! C'est tres amusant!*"

"What?" Holly asked.

In reply the boy ran up the steps, sat on the banister, and came flying down, his hands in mid-air.

"*Alors*," the French-speaking boy said, "*essayez-le!*"

From his gestures Ricky realized what he meant. Ricky ran to the top of the flight of steps with the two girls following. Perching on the railing, he held on lightly with one hand as he slid to the bottom.

"This is great!" he exclaimed as the children laughed and clapped.

"I'll bet I can do it with no hands," Holly called.

"Bet you can't," Ricky teased.

"All right then. Watch this."

Holly sat on the rail. Then, holding her arms out like a bird's wings in flight, she started to zip down. But as she reached the bottom, pigtails flying, Holly was going so fast she could not stop herself.

"Oh!" she cried out in dismay.

At the foot of the stairs a workman was hurrying along, a lunch pail under his arm. Holly zipped off the banister and—*wham!*—she sailed right into the startled workman.

The lunch pail flew into the air, and both the man and the little girl tumbled to the ground. The pail landed with a *smack*, opened, and four sandwiches spilled onto the snowy ground.

"*Qu'est-ce qui se passe?*" the man cried out.

"Oh, I'm so sorry," Holly said. She picked herself

off the ground, then helped the workman retrieve his sandwiches. Sue ran quickly down the steps.

He sputtered volubly in French, which was translated for the Hollisters by a woman passing by.

"What is he saying?" Ricky asked.

"That he must hurry or he will miss the ferryboat to Levis."

"Where's that?" Holly asked.

"On the other side of the river," the woman said, pointing.

"Oh, we're so, so sorry, Mr.——"

Seeing that the children were frightened and sorry, the man managed a grin. "I Victor Tremblay," he said.

"What!"

"Oh, don't go away!"

"We want to talk to you!"

The three children were so excited they could hardly get the words out quickly enough.

"We've found you! We've found you!" Holly said, pulling at the man's sleeve.

A crowd gathered to watch the excitement. Among them was a woman teacher on her way to the local school. She, too, offered her services as a translator. A halting conversation went on between the three young Hollisters and the French-Canadian.

"We're looking for a Victor Tremblay," Holly said. "He can solve our mystery." Quickly she told

Holly sailed into the workman.

about the missing *cariole*. "Please, where is it, Mr. Tremblay?"

In reply the man shrugged and talked fast. The teacher translated. "There are sixty thousand Tremblays in Quebec Province and Victors enough to fill the St. Lawrence! I'm not the man you want, but good luck in your search."

The Hollisters looked glum and turned away, just as Gram and Gramp came hurrying up to them with Pete and Pam.

"So here you are!" Pam cried out. "We thought you were lost!"

"Lucky the policeman told us where you went," Pete said.

Just then Victor Tremblay looked in panic toward the ferry slip several blocks away.

"Oh, he's going to miss his ferry," Holly said sympathetically. "And it's all my fault."

Hearing what had happened, Gramp Hollister hailed a cab. Taking Sue, Holly, and Victor Tremblay with him he rode to the ferry slip as the others followed on foot.

"*Merci! Merci!*" Mr. Tremblay said as he left them and dashed onto the boat.

The ferry had left by the time the other Hollisters arrived, but they could see a sister ship steaming across the river from Levis. The family watched it arrive, then Ricky begged for a trip across the St. Lawrence.

"We're right here," Gramp said, "so we may as well do it."

When the others agreed, Pete bought tickets for all of them. They hurried up the gangplank with the milling crowd of working people on their way to Levis. Gram held Holly's hand while Pam and Gramp took charge of Sue. Once on the deck, the older Hollisters started looking for Pete and Ricky, who were not in sight.

"Where are the two boys?" Gram asked worriedly as the ferryboat with a toot started off across the ice-choked river.

"Maybe they didn't get on the ferry after all," Pam said.

She peered among the crowd, hoping to locate her two brothers, but they were nowhere in sight.

"Oh, Gram," she said fearfully, "do you suppose Pete and Ricky did miss the boat?"

The ferry now was making fast time toward the middle of the river. The Hollisters gazed back at the city, which loomed proudly from the top of the huge wall. The hotel in particular stood out like a medieval castle.

Suddenly Sue shouted, "I see them! I see them!"

"Where? Who?" Pam asked.

"The boys. Way up there!"

CHAPTER 7

VANISHED

ALL eyes turned to the top of the cliff.

"Oh!" Gram said. "How could Pete and Ricky have run up there so fast?"

Sue giggled. "No, no," she said. "I mean they're on top of the boat!"

The boys were standing on the bridge beside the captain.

"Pete! Ricky!" their grandmother called.

Hearing her, they waved, and Pete shouted, "We'd like to ask the captain to let us steer the ferry, but he doesn't speak English!"

"Use sign language," Pam called back with a grin.

Pete and Ricky followed her advice, pointing first to the big steering wheel, then to themselves, and finally to the dock on the other side of the river. At last the captain, a short, youthful-looking man in a blue uniform, got their idea.

"*Oui, oui,*" he said, and motioned Ricky to the wheel.

The boy turned it one way, then the other, making the boat zigzag a little before the captain assisted him. Next it was Pete's turn.

"Crickets! This is fun!" he said. But as he steered a huge ice floe drifted directly into the path of the ferryboat. "What do I do now?" he asked the captain, worried.

The Canadian put his hand on the wheel, easing it to the left, but not in time to avoid the chunk of river ice.

Crunch! The boat brushed against it and shuddered a little. At this point the captain took over again.

"*Pardon,*" Pete said, grinning sheepishly, and Ricky added, "Mercy buckets." The pilot laughed.

Both boys marveled at his skill as he warped the ferryboat against the side of the dock at Levis. The gangplank was let down, and automobiles and passengers quickly streamed off the ferry. Gram, Gramp, and the girls were left alone on the deck beneath where the boys were standing. "Come on up!" Pete called down. "You get a great view of Quebec from here!"

Ricky pointed out a stairway leading up to the wheelhouse, and the three ascended just as passengers and cars were loading for the return trip. Among them was a *padre,* dressed in a black coat and hat. He came to the top deck and faced across the river to admire the inspiring scene of the old French citadel.

With the ferryboat loaded again the captain tooted his whistle, then backed out into the river.

As the wind blew into the Hollisters' faces, Holly tugged at Gramp's coat sleeve. "Oh, look!" she said. "Isn't that funny!"

"What, dear?"

"The river is running backward," she said in amazement.

"It sure is!" Pete exclaimed. "Only a while ago it was running toward the ocean!"

"We must be seeing things," Ricky said, shoving back his hat and revealing his red head.

Hearing this, the *padre* smiled and turned to them. "No, you are not seeing things," he said in perfect English. "The river is running backward. The tide is coming in from the sea now."

The *padre* explained that in Quebec the tide reached a height of eighteen feet.

"Oh!" Sue remarked. "The St. Lawrence is an up and down river, isn't it?" The others laughed.

After chatting with the man for a while, the Hollister girls said they would like to steer the boat too. The *padre* kindly translated their request to the captain who gladly assented. Sue tried it first for a few moments, then Holly, and finally Pam guided the ferry past an ice floe, missing it by a few feet.

As the captain took over again, Holly said, "Ha, ha! We didn't hit any ice!" She looked directly at Pete and winked.

Arriving at Quebec once more, the Hollisters debarked, said good-by to the friendly *padre*, and hurried out onto the snow-filled street at the foot of the river.

"Now let's start our sleuthing," Pete begged.

"I'm hungry!" Sue interrupted.

Since it was nearly noontime, they ate a snack at a nearby restaurant, then hailed a sleigh driver to take them to the address of Victor Tremblay.

With Holly and Sue seated on the laps of Gram and Gramp they squeezed into the large open sleigh. The driver threw a bearskin rug over their knees. The horse pulled them slowly along the narrow streets of the old city, then up the hill.

Finally they came to the street on which Victor Tremblay lived. The driver stopped in front of a quaint red-brick house.

"This is the place," Pam said, noting the address, and volunteered, "I'll knock on the door."

She stepped down from the sleigh, traversed a small path cut into the snowbank and stopped before the green front door. She knocked several times. The door opened a crack, and an elderly woman with a shawl around her shoulders peered out.

"Is this the home of Victor Tremblay?"

"Is this the home of Victor Tremblay?" Pam asked.

"It is," the old woman said in halting English. "I mean, it *was.*"

"Doesn't he live here any more?" Pam asked.

"Sorry," the woman replied. "Victor Tremblay became ill in December. There was no one to take care of him, so he went to stay with relatives."

"Where?" Pam asked eagerly.

The old woman shook her head. "That I do not know," she said.

"Didn't he leave an address?"

"No. He said he was going somewhere up the river."

A surge of disappointment took hold of Pam. "Thank you, *merci,*" she said to the woman, who made a little bow and closed the door.

When Pam told the others what she had learned they sat for a moment in stunned silence.

"What'll we do now?" Ricky asked.

Pete thought for a while, then said, "I have an idea. If Victor Tremblay made sleighs, he certainly must have purchased paint and fittings at hardware stores. Let's ask at some of them."

Gramp Hollister agreed that Pete's idea might produce a clue. The driver was ordered to take them to the closest hardware and paint stores. First one, then another, and finally the third merchant said that they knew Victor Tremblay well but they had not seen him for several months.

"Sorry, we cannot help you," the third merchant said with a gesture of his hands. "But I wish you luck."

By now Ricky, Holly, and Sue had grown weary of sleuthing and wanted to return to the hotel.

"You promised us a ride on the toboggan, Gram," Sue said. "Please take us."

"Me too," chimed in Holly.

"Same here," Ricky added. "Boy, that toboggan is neat."

Pete and Pam, although discouraged at the moment, begged to continue with their detective work.

"All right," Gramp said. "Suppose Gram and I take the three younger ones to the toboggan while you two continue the search."

Pete and Pam stepped out of the sleigh and, with a map of Quebec in their hands, started off, promising to be back in time for supper. When the others reached the hotel, the sleigh stopped and Gramp paid the driver.

Sue, out first, raced ahead toward the toboggan run. She glanced up at the slide. It was clear. The little girl began climbing over the three icy grooves to get to the other side.

Just then a toboggan carrying two children started from the top of the run.

Ricky, running along behind his sister, saw this. "Hurry, Sue! Hurry!" he cried out. But the little girl's earmuffs and the whistling wind prevented her from hearing the warning.

Terrified, Ricky dashed forward, leaped over the first two chutes, and gave his sister a big push. Together the children rolled out of the way just as the toboggan zipped past them.

Several onlookers caught their breaths, then gasped with relief when they saw that Sue and Ricky were safe. When Gram and Gramp caught up to them they praised the boy for his heroism and made Sue promise never to do such a thing again.

"I'm sorry," Sue said, wiping away a tear.

"All's well that ends well," Ricky said importantly, repeating what he had often heard grownups say, and added, "May we have a ride now, Gramp?"

"The safest place on this slide," Gram said, looking at the chutes, "is on the toboggan itself. You may try a run."

It was a long steep climb to the top of the hill. When they reached it the children took their places on a toboggan. As they held onto one another tightly, Holly glanced down the slope. "Ooh!" she said. "This is scary, isn't it?"

"The scarier, the better," Ricky said. "Here we go!"

Down they went, at first slowly then gaining momentum. The speed and the wind made their faces tingle, and they shouted gleefully. The toboggan reached the foot of the slide and glided along, slowing to a stop.

Before it came to a halt the three youngsters aboard saw Pete and Pam running toward them waving their arms. "We found a clue! We found a clue!" Pam shouted.

CHAPTER 8

A SURPRISE FOR PETE

HARDLY able to wait for the toboggan to stop before telling their news, Pete and Pam raced beside it, shouting, "We think we've found Victor Tremblay!"

"Oh boy!" said Ricky. "Now we——" He stopped short in amazement as Gram and Gramp whizzed down the adjacent slide, jumped off, and came to join the children.

"Guess what!" said Pete. "We know where Victor Tremblay is!"

He and Pam had visited another shopkeeper. The man had heard that Victor Tremblay, the sleigh maker, had gone to Baie St. Paul.

"Look," Pete said, unfolding the map. "Here's where it is." His finger pointed to a dot representing a town on the St. Lawrence River about sixty miles nearer to the mouth than Quebec.

"And see here," Pam added, "there's a large island in the river opposite Baie St. Paul. Its name is Ile aux Coudres."

"Oh yes," Gramp said. "It's a pleasant drive to Baie St. Paul. A good road all the way."

"Then may we go right away?" Ricky asked.

"Tomorrow, if the weather is good," their grandfather replied. "It's too late to set out now. Let's enjoy the tobogganing. Pete and Pam, you take a couple of turns."

As Pam climbed the slope she wondered how many Tremblays lived at Baie St. Paul. Pete pondered whether the sleigh maker might have gone to Ile aux Coudres.

After several more slides, the Hollisters went back to the hotel. They changed their clothes, then went downstairs to dinner.

Everyone ordered steaming hot onion soup. How delicious it tasted! For the main course Pete and Gramp tried frogs' legs. The others had *Pompano en papillote*, a fillet of pompano fish stuffed with shrimp and lobster and baked in little containers of parchment paper. Sue was intrigued by the "paper dishes" as she called them.

"They are the papillotes," explained her grandmother.

When the meal was over their waiter brought them a little tray with a white doily. On it were little candy snowmen representing *Bonhomme Carnaval*.

"Oh, aren't they cute!" Holly giggled as she took hers and said, "*Merci*."

The candy figure had a purple hat and blue eyes, a red nose and mouth, beneath which were two blue buttons and a sash of purple and blue.

"He looks so jolly!" Pam said, laughing as she bit off her snowman's head.

Speaking with an accent, their waiter said, "Ah yes, they are what you call a 'heet' with children who dine here."

"Oh, a hit," Pete said, smiling. "No wonder. They taste good too."

Just then the headwaiter, a tall handsome man with a mustache, stepped over to the Hollisters' table. "I'm glad you like them," he said. "We make them in our own kitchens."

Holly smiled up at him. "May we see how you make them?" she asked.

The man bowed and said, "*Oui.* If you would like, I would be happy to show you. The chef is not busy at the moment."

Gram and Gramp said they would stay to sip their coffee while the children went to visit the kitchen. They followed the headwaiter, whose name was Mr. Blanc. He turned and smiled. "We will go on a grand tour of the kitchen," he said.

Pushing through swinging doors, they entered a spotless white-tiled room. Delicious odors came from many kettles steaming on the stoves.

"Here is where our onion soup is made," Mr. Blanc

said. One of the chefs reached in with a wooden ladle to stir the contents of the giant kettle.

"And here," Mr. Blanc said as he walked along, "is our potato masher."

"Yikes!" Ricky cried. "It looks like a washing machine."

"Yes, the old-fashioned type," Pam remarked.

Inside the creamy white potatoes were being churned by revolving ladles. "And now," Mr. Blanc said, walking down the aisle to a smaller room, "This is Mr. Carteau, our pastry and candy chef." He introduced the children to a small rotund man with a curly mustache. He wore a very high chef's cap.

"They would like to see you make some *Bonhommes Carnavals*," Mr. Blanc said.

"Weeth pleasure," the man replied. "I am just making some more now. Come, see."

Adjusting his white apron more firmly over his ample waist, the chef led the children to a long table on which he had just finished molding the white bodies of the snowmen. "Maybe the young ladies would like to put on the decorations?" he suggested.

"Oh yes!" Pam replied.

The chef picked up a piece of waxed paper, twirled it deftly in his fingers, forming a cone. Into this he poured some warm red frosting, then folded over the wide end of the cone. He handed this to Pam.

"You make the nose, the mouth, and one strand of the belt," he said, smiling.

Gingerly, Pam took the piping tube in her hand and gently squeezed it. Soon half a dozen *Bonhommes Carnavals* had noses, mouths, and waistbands. Then Mr. Carteau handed another tube to Holly. "You make the blue eyes," he said.

Squirt, squirt, squirt! The blue eyes were ready. "And now a blue strip for the belt," said the pastry chef. Holly deftly followed instructions, giggling all the while.

"What do I do?" Sue chirped up.

"You will put on the *chapeau*," said the chef.

"The what?"

"The hat."

"Oh," Sue said as she took a tube of purple icing. The chef showed her how to give the flowing icing a little twist which provided a rakish tilt to the candy hat. The first hat Sue made was almost as big as *Bonhomme Carnaval* himself. The others laughed when they saw it.

"Not so much squeeze," Mr. Carteau said, shaking his finger.

The next hat was perfect, and before long each snowman wore one.

"I'd like to try that too," Ricky said. "But there's nothing more to do."

Pete smiled and said, "I think there is."

"What?"
"Shoes."
Hearing this the chef smiled. "We have not been putting shoes on *Bonhomme Carnaval,* but if you like——" He made a flourish with his right hand. "Try it."
"What color?" Ricky asked.
"How about red?" Pam suggested.
"Red shoes it is," said Ricky as the chef handed him the piping bag.
The boy's attempt to put shoes on the snowman proved to be a great success, if one should judge by the size.
"Crickets! They're seven-league boots!" exclaimed Pete as Ricky squirted great globs of icing on *Bonhomme Carnaval's* feet.
But even when the freckle-faced lad tried to apply shoes a few sizes smaller, the effect still was generous.
"Oh well," he said, finishing the job, "these snowmen are different, anyway!"
"You can say that again," Pam said, laughing.
In a few minutes the candies were ready to be lifted off the table. Ricky helped himself to the one with the largest boots.
"Now let's see how *Bonhomme Carnaval* can travel in his seven-league boots," Ricky exclaimed. Holding the figure between his fingers, the boy made the

Ricky attempted to put shoes on the snowman.

snowman leap from pot to pot. But when he reached the giant potato masher, *plop! Bonhomme* fell into it.

"Hey! Wait!" Ricky cried out. He peered down into the mashing potatoes. At first he saw the candy snowman being churned back and forth. Then it fell apart and disappeared into the fluffy whiteness.

Ricky's brother and sisters looked frightened until the head waiter hurried over to the potato masher, laughing. "No harm done," he said. "In fact, I think the potatoes needed a dash of sugar anyway."

"You mean nobody will know the difference?" Pam asked.

"If anybody does," Mr. Blanc went on, "we'll simply tell him these are potatoes *au Hollister*—something new on our menu." The children laughed and felt relieved.

"What'll we do with the other snowmen?" Sue asked the kindly headwaiter.

"What do you want to do with them?" Mr. Blanc asked Pete.

"Eat them."

"But first let's take them to show Gram and Gramp," Pam spoke up.

"And let's send some to our friends," Holly suggested. "Jeff and Anne Hunter and Donna Martin."

The chef wrapped the *Bonhommes Carnavals* in waxed paper, then packed them in small boxes. The Happy Hollister children thanked him and Mr. Blanc for the tour of the kitchen and returned to the dining room. On their way out Mr. Blanc handed each a little plastic figure.

"More *Bonhommes Carnavals!*" Ricky said as he attached his tiny snowman to a buttonhole.

"You must carry these when you walk about Quebec," Mr. Blanc said, smiling. "Otherwise you'll get a very big surprise."

"Why?" Ricky asked, tilting his head.

"You wait and see," Mr. Blanc said.

When they reached the lobby, Sue was so sleepy she would hardly walk and tugged at her grandmother's arm.

"I think I'll mail these packages to your friends, then take Sue up to bed," Gram Hollister said.

"Can't we stay up longer?" Holly begged. She glanced outside and saw that it had grown dark. The town was sparkling with lights again.

Gramp volunteered to take the children for a walk to see the sights. When they put on their coats each made sure that his *Bonhomme Carnaval* was dangling from a coat button.

The Hollisters walked down the street. Soon they heard music in the distance.

"More dancers," Holly said. "I want to see them." She ran on ahead.

The others followed the sound of music to a great

square and Pete looked up at a sign. "Duval Square," he said. "I've heard of this place."

It was brightly lighted and full of dancing figures. Another ice palace, larger than the first one they had seen, towered over the revelers in the center of the square. There was a policeman stationed at the door of the palace, and inside the children could see several laughing young people who seemed to be buying souvenirs from a clown. A loudspeaker, mounted high on a pole, blared forth popular tunes which the children knew well.

Getting into the spirit of the fun, Pete danced with Pam and Ricky with Holly. Back and forth, around and around they went. Suddenly, however, a group of laughing boys and girls surrounded Pete. They spoke to him rapidly in French.

Pete grinned. "Crickets! I don't know what you're trying to say," he told them.

Hearing him speak English, one of the girls giggled and said, "You must come away with us."

They took Pete by the hand and pulled him through the crowd, laughing gaily.

"Where are they taking him?" Pam cried out.

Nearby a policeman grinned at the scene. Hearing Pam's remark, he said, "The boy must go to jail!"

CHAPTER 9

THE RUNAWAY

HEARING that their brother must go to jail, Ricky and Holly became frightened.

"Come on, Ricky," Holly said, tugging at her brother. "Let's get Gramp. He can help us."

The policeman, noticing that the younger children were worried, bent down to speak to them. "Nothing bad is going to happen to your brother," he said kindly, "but you see, he is not wearing a *Bonhomme Carnaval.*"

Pete looked at his jacket. The little plastic snowman was gone!

"You must have lost him while we were dancing," Pam said.

If the little mascot had fallen into the snow, by now the figure had been trampled by hundreds of dancing feet and Pete realized it would be impossible to find it.

"*Venez avec nous, venez avec nous!*" the Quebec children chanted as they pulled Pete toward the Ice

Palace. Unafraid now, the Hollisters joined the spirit of the fun. Laughing gaily they followed Pete to the portals of the icy "jail." There they were faced by the clown and several prisoners.

"Where is your *Bonhomme Carnaval?*" the clown asked, grinning broadly.

"I lost it," Pete replied, suppressing a grin. "I'm sorry."

Just then Holly cried out, "Pete, I have one!"

"What?"

"A candy snowman. See!" She put her hand inside her dress pocket and pulled out one of the *Bonhommes Carnavals* which they had decorated in the hotel kitchen.

Pete took it and held the candy up to the clown. "Will this do?" he asked.

"Fine!" the clown replied. "You are now freed!" Then he added with a wink, "Since you are a guest of Quebec, we were going to give you another one anyhow."

The other prisoners were not so fortunate. They had to pay twenty-five cents apiece to buy another snowman so they could be freed to rejoin the rollicking crowd.

When the children joined Gramp again, he said, "Well, I guess this is enough excitement for one evening," and they all hurried back to the hotel.

Preparations for the trip to Baie St. Paul got under

way the next morning. Gram packed pajamas and extra clothing into two overnight bags in case they should not return to Quebec that night. By midmorning the Hollisters were on their way. They rode through the narrow streets of Quebec and finally crossed a bridge. Then Gramp set off on a broad highway paralleling the St. Lawrence River.

"I have a feeling," Pam said, "that this will be a day of surprises."

"I think it will too," Gram agreed, "and the first surprise is coming soon."

"What is that?" Pete asked.

Gram told them that they soon would see the beautiful cathedral of Ste. Anne de Beaupré, one of the popular tourist attractions of French Canada.

"It's right up ahead," Gramp said finally, as he turned off to the left and stopped before the cathedral.

"May we go in and look around?" Pam asked.

"Of course," Gram said. "This is a shrine where crippled people come, hoping to be cured. Many leave their crutches and go away able to walk without them."

After the children had viewed the beautiful works of art they stood in awe at sight of the stacks of canes and crutches. Then they returned to the car.

Farther along the road Ricky saw a road sign and chuckled. "What a funny name! St. Tite des

Caps." He pronounced it "tight-de-caps." "Somebody around here must have had a cap that was too tight."

"Oh, stop it!" Pam protested, making a face at her brother. "Gram, you should say 'St. Teet des Caps,' shouldn't you?"

"That's right."

Gramp drove into a small town which was little more than a cluster of stores with a few houses on either side of the main road. He had to slow to a crawl because of heavy traffic which consisted mainly of horse-drawn sleighs.

Pete suddenly cried out, "There's a *cariole* just like the one we're looking for!"

The sleigh, drawn by a single horse, stood in front of the general store. Gramp pulled over to the side of the road as soon as he found a space and stopped the car so they could get a good view of the *cariole*.

"Oh, maybe it's ours!" Holly cried out, standing up to look back.

A bearskin rug, which the owner had apparently tossed over the front of the sleigh, concealed the place where the letters "H.H." might have been written. Before any of the Hollisters had a chance to run back, two small boys and a girl climbed into the *cariole* and pulled the rug onto their laps. One boy picked up the reins, and the horse started.

There were no initials on the sleigh. "It's not our *cariole* after all," said Pete with a sigh.

Gramp, about to pull onto the road again, honked his horn. The sudden noise caused the horse to bolt. With a jerk on the reins which pulled them from the boy's hands, the horse broke into a gallop, his head held high. The *cariole* swayed from side to side behind him.

"We must help those children!" Pam cried out as her grandfather stopped the car.

Pete leaped out. As the horse dashed by he reached up and seized the dangling reins. Although the boy tried to pull the horse to a halt, he was not equal to the animal's strength. The horse pulled Pete off balance and dragged him along the snowy street. But Pete's weight finally brought the runaway to a halt as a crowd gathered.

Most frightened of all were the three children in the sleigh. With guilty looks on their faces they thanked Pete in French.

Just then a man ran from the store, waving his arms wildly. He scolded the three French children until tears came to their eyes.

"What's he saying?" Sue asked her grandmother.

Gram Hollister whispered that the youngsters had taken the sleigh without permission while the owner was in the store.

Pete tried to pull the horse to a halt.

"But they promised never to do such a thing again," she said.

Though Holly knew the children had been wrong, still she felt sorry for them. "They didn't mean to hurt anything," she said.

"That's right," Pete agreed. "And besides, it was our fault that the horse got scared."

"I'd like to buy the children some cookies in that bakery over there," said Holly.

When the scared-looking youngsters heard this in French from Gram, their faces broke into shining smiles. With the Hollisters they trooped into the bake-shop, where sugar cookies were purchased for every-one.

As they stood around eating them Ricky said, "Do you remember the time Domingo ran away and wrecked our cart between two trees?"

"I sure do," Pete answered.

Suddenly there was silence among the Hollisters. Poor Domingo! Was their pet still missing or had he been found? For a moment each child wished he might be home about five minutes to find out.

As Gramp paid the baker for the cookies he asked the proprietor, "Where's the best place to eat at Baie St. Paul?"

"Hotel Eau Clair," the baker replied. "It is near the river front. You can't miss it."

The Hollisters and the little French children, still

munching on their cookies, waved good-by. Then Gramp started again for the river town. It was shortly after noon when he pulled up in front of the hotel, which was really an old farmhouse. It looked out over the St. Lawrence River and Ile aux Coudres.

At the rear of the hotel Pete noticed a bright red single-motor airplane on a snow-covered runway. He said, "Come on!" to the others and dashed around the building.

"Yikes!" Ricky cried out. "The plane has skis instead of wheels!"

"It must be fun to ride in a ski airplane!" said Holly.

"I wonder who owns it?" Pam remarked as the children went back to Gram and Gramp and climbed the porch steps of the hotel.

The Hollisters were met at the door by a pretty, dark-haired woman who introduced herself as Mrs. La Fontaine. At her side was a little boy who she said was her son Jacques.

"He does not speak such good English yet," Mrs. La Fontaine said as the Hollisters removed their wraps.

"How old are you?" Holly asked Jacques.

The boy smiled at her. "Six o'clock," he said.

The Hollisters chuckled at this, and the little boy blushed. Pam said quickly. "*We* can't speak any French at all. I think you're doing very well."

This made Jacques feel better. "I mean I am six years old," he said, "and I'm a blueberry too."

"Oh dear," Mrs. La Fontaine said as she led the guests into the dining room. "Jacques will tell you his whole history before long."

"What is a blueberry?" Pete asked as he held a chair for Gram Hollister.

Mrs. La Fontaine explained that blueberry was a name given to the people who came from the Lake St. John area where blueberries were grown.

"I'm glad I'm a blueberry," Jacques said.

"May I eat you?" Holly teased. With that Jacques disappeared into the kitchen while the Hollisters looked over the luncheon menu.

While they were being served by Mrs. La Fontaine, she told them something about the restaurant. The family had come from Lake St. John where Mr. La Fontaine was a pilot for sportsmen. The red airplane belonged to him.

Hearing this, Pam spoke up, "Mr. La Fontaine must know many people around here," she said. "Perhaps you can help us."

"Of course. What is it?"

"We're trying to find a man named Victor Tremblay," Pam continued. "Do you know him?"

"Victor Tremblay?" the woman repeated, rolling her eyes upward thoughtfully. Then she added, "Oh yes. Victor Tremblay went to Ile aux Coudres. That means Hazelnut Island, you know."

Mrs. La Fontaine said that the sleigh maker had gone there to recuperate from an illness. He was staying at the home of his five cousins.

"They're brothers and all rivermen," she explained. "The cousins are entered in the canoe race at Quebec next Sunday. The Tremblays have a fine chance of winning."

The Hollisters were so excited to hear this they could hardly finish their delicious meal.

"We must get to the island right away," Pete urged.

"How will we do it?" Ricky piped up. "Is there a ferryboat?"

"Only in the summertime," Mrs. La Fontaine said. "But my husband could fly you over."

"Fine!" said Grandfather Hollister. "We may clear up this mystery of ours today."

Mrs. La Fontaine called to her husband, who was in the attic. He came down immediately. Mr. La Fontaine was a medium-sized, stocky man with a jutting chin and clear blue eyes. The children liked him at once.

The pilot explained that he was also a radio ham. "My short-wave sets are in the attic," he said. "Would you boys like to see them?"

"Oh yes."

Pete and Ricky followed him to the small attic room. On a table against one wall stood all kinds of radio equipment: a sending set with dials and knobs and a receiving unit with a large speaker.

"Would you send a message?" Ricky asked him. "I'd like to watch."

Obligingly Mr. La Fontaine did as requested. The sending set crackled and snapped, but in a few moments an answer came back over the receiving section.

"That's neat!" said Ricky, and Pete nodded his enthusiasm. "I wish we had one of these."

As the group went downstairs Pete explained that the Hollisters wanted to fly to Ile aux Coudres.

"I'll take you," the pilot said. "But I can accommodate only three passengers at a time. How about 'ladies first?' "

The prospect of a take-off on skis sent a thrill down the children's spines. Pete helped Gram in first and then Sue, Holly, and Pam. The pilot twirled the propeller, and the engine took hold. Mr. La Fontaine hopped inside the plane. The bright red craft started off over the snow, gathered speed, and finally rose, heading out over the St. Lawrence.

Half an hour later Mr. La Fontaine returned. "Hop in, folks," he said to Gramp and the boys.

When they had taken their seats he started off again, whizzing down the slippery runway.

As he took to the air, Ricky's eyes grew large. "We're climbing fast!"

Mr. La Fontaine adjusted the trim tab with a small wheel overhead. The boys meanwhile were gazing down into the St. Lawrence River, which was filled with giant ice floes. The island was coming plainly into view when suddenly the motor sputtered, then died.

"Oh!" the boys exclaimed.

The pilot nosed the plane down so as not to lose flying speed. "I'm afraid we can't make it to the island!" he called back above the whistling wind.

"Where will we land?" Pete asked, worried.

"On an ice floe."

CHAPTER 10

A PUP NAMED POILU

After circling over the ice floes, the pilot nosed the plane down into a steep glide and headed for the largest chunk floating in the river. The Hollister boys' pulses pounded with excitement as the red airplane skimmed low.

Finally the skis touched down on the ice floe which was covered with several inches of soft snow. Less than halfway across the giant mass the plane came to a halt. The pilot hopped out, tinkered with the motor a moment, and called back:

"The gaz line is clogged."

"Does he mean gas?" Ricky asked his grandfather.

Gramp Hollister nodded. "The French spell it *gaz*."

"Can you fix it?" Pete called out.

"I think so, if you will please hand me those wrenches under my seat."

Pete did this, and the pilot went to work. After removing a small metal hose, he put one end to his lips and blew into it.

"Now she's clear," he said, and quickly replaced the hose.

Mr. La Fontaine then climbed back into the plane. After adjusting the controls he stepped out again and spun the propeller. The motor started with a rackety roar.

Back in his seat the pilot smiled and said, "Here we go."

He turned the plane around and taxied to the opposite end of the ice floe. Then, maneuvering into position, he once more headed into the wind.

With the motor roaring, the craft raced over the soft snow and near the other end of the floe lifted into the air.

Everyone breathed a sigh of relief, and Ricky shouted, "Hurray, we're safe!"

The pilot wore a serious look, however, until they had gained altitude. Then he broke into a smile, banked his plane, and pointed to the end of the island.

"That's a famous landmark," he said.

"The old windmill?"

"Yes. I will fly low so you can see it."

The boys and Gramp fixed their eyes on the old French provincial windmill as the pilot came closer.

"They say it looks just like the ones in France," he told the Hollisters as they flew past it.

A short distance away Mr. La Fontaine brought the plane down in a snow-covered cornfield. Then he taxied up to a snowmobile where Gram, Holly, Sue, and Pam were waiting for them.

"I don't like to fly after dark," the pilot said to Gramp. "It shouldn't take you long to find the Tremblays, so if you're not back here in an hour I'll assume you're staying over night. I'll come back for you tomorrow afternoon."

Gramp Hollister agreed to this and turned to the snowmobile. The vehicle had tank treads instead of wheels and inside a long bench on either side.

The driver did not speak English, so Mr. La Fontaine ordered him to drive the Hollisters to the home of a man who did. "He'll take you to a Mr.Mailloux," the pilot said. "He'll be able to direct you to the Tremblays' farm."

With their two overnight bags securely beside them, the Hollisters joggled and bounced over the stubby cornfield until they came to a dirt road. There the driver turned into a rutted trail until he came to a small farmhouse set far back in an open field.

With more grinding and bouncing, the snowmobile was pulled up in front of the door. An old man with a short, cropped beard opened the door and stepped out. After an exchange of French words with the driver he introduced himself as Mr. Mailloux.

"Come in," he invited. "Rest awhile, and I will tell you where the Tremblays live."

He asked the driver to wait, then ushered the Hollisters into a small living room. It was furnished with very old chairs and a table.

"I hear you have come from Quebec," the elderly man said, seating himself in a straight-backed chair.

"Yes," Holly said. "Have you ever been there?"

"Ah yes, fifty years ago," he replied. "I went to Quebec to buy myself a horse. But the big city—— *Ma foi!* I could not bear it! So I came back to my island and I have not been off it since."

The visitors were amazed to hear that anyone could remain in the same small place for such a long time. But in further conversation with Mr. Mailloux they learned that many people on Ile aux Coudres had never been to the mainland.

"We like it here. God is good to us. He gives us crops of fine apples," said their host. "So why should we go elsewhere?"

As he spoke, the children heard a small scratching sound. Turning their heads, they saw a small dog peering around the corner of the kitchen door.

"*Poilu!*" Mr. Mailloux called out. "Come meet my guests."

The little dog bounded into the room and hopped onto his master's lap.

"Oh, isn't he cute!" Pam exclaimed, reaching over to pet the little smooth-haired terrier.

"Yes, *Poilu* is my friend. And he can do tricks," the old man said. "Watch."

He stood up and reached for his fur cap which hung on a peg beside the door. Then, putting it on, he returned to his chair. Instantly *Poilu* jumped to his master's lap, then to his shoulder and, to the delight of the children, pulled the hat from his master's head.

"See, *Poilu* knows that I should be polite and not wear my hat in the house," Mr. Mailloux said.

"Will he do the same for us?" Holly asked.

The old man laughed. "Try it."

Holly put on her own hat and sat on the floor. Immediately *Poilu* put his front paws on her shoulder and took off her hat, giving three little barks.

"He's a trick dog!" Sue cried out. Then she added, "Our dog Zip at home can do tricks too. Only he's much larger."

The children took turns letting the little dog remove their hats. Then the conversation turned to the Tremblays and the missing Victor.

"Yes, Victor has been on our island for several months," the farmer said. He rose and went to a window, pointing out a farmhouse half a mile down the

"Poilu knows I should'nt wear my hat."

road. "There's where the brothers live," he said. "They are bachelors."

"Oh dear," Pam said kindly. "Don't they have anyone to cook for them?"

"Indeed they do," Mr. Mailloux replied. "Their aunt, Tante Cecile, and she is devoted to them."

He told the Hollisters that the Tremblays' aunt had kept house for the husky rivermen many years. "She speaks a little English, so you should have no trouble," he added.

All this time Ricky's eyes had been roving around the room. Suddenly he noticed something which made him curious. A strange-looking object which resembled a gravy boat with a handle attached to a metal bracket hung on the wall.

"What's that?" Ricky asked.

Mr. Mailloux chuckled. "This is the oldest object on our island," he said. "It's an oil lamp brought over by the Frenchmen who originally settled here."

"I didn't know people had oil in those days," Pete remarked.

"They used porpoise oil," Mr. Mailloux explained. He told them that these interesting mammals swam up the St. Lawrence River and were caught in traps. "They provided fine oil for our ancestors' lamps," he said, taking the lamp down and handing it to Ricky.

The boy turned the lamp in his hands. Then as he

started to pass it to Pam, suddenly the lamp slipped from his grasp!

"Oh!" he cried. Bending quickly, he managed to catch the old oil lamp before it reached the floor.

"Yikes!" he exclaimed. "I nearly——"

"No harm done," the old man said, taking the lamp and showing it to the other children.

As they were about to leave his house, Mr. Mailloux added, "Wait! I have a surprise for you."

"Pam, you were right," said Sue. "This *is* a day of surprises."

The farmer disappeared into the kitchen and returned a moment later with a bowl full of fragrant red apples. He gave one to each visitor, saying, "Come back sometime and see me."

"We'd love to," Holly said. "We'd like to play with *Poilu* too."

The Hollisters stuffed the apples into their pockets and climbed into the snowmobile once more. After Mr. Mailloux had given the driver directions, they set off and soon pulled up in front of the Tremblays' home.

Gramp tried to pay the driver, but the Frenchman shook his head and smilingly protested, "*Non, non,*" and added in French, "Thank you, but you are guests on our island."

When Gram translated this for the children they

all cried, "*Merci, merci!*" as he waved and drove off.

Pete knocked on the door. When it opened a small, elderly lady, with red cheeks wrinkled like long-stored apples, stood there, smiling.

Gram was first to speak. "You are Tante Cecile?" she asked.

"*Oui,*" the woman replied, blinking her bright blue eyes as if trying to determine who the callers were.

Grandmother Hollister soon put the old lady at ease as she introduced herself, her husband, and her grandchildren.

"We are looking for a Victor Tremblay," Gramp added. "Is he here?"

"Come inside," Tante Cecile said. "Nobody is home now, but they will all be back soon."

When Pete stepped inside the house with the others he glanced about with wide-eyed curiosity. This was not like homes he had seen in the United States. The downstairs, instead of being divided into rooms, was one big single area.

At the back of the spacious room was a wood-burning stove, and to one side stood a dining table. The front of the room contained an overstuffed sofa, several large chairs, and an ancient piano. But what a fresh, sweet aroma the place had!

Before they removed any wraps, Gram explained

their mission and added, "I think the children would rather play outside for a while. May they?"

"Of course," Tante Cecile replied. Then she took a heavy coat from beside the door and put it over her shoulders.

"*Venez*, come," she said. "I will show you our birds."

"Chickens?" Holly asked as they trooped out of the house and around to the back.

"They are chickens to us," the woman replied. "You will see presently."

Soon the group came to what looked like a chicken coop with a wire run, but the birds inside were not chickens.

Pam stopped short and cried out, "Pheasants! Aren't they beautiful! Do you raise them, Tante Cecile?"

The woman answered "Yes." Pheasants were easy to breed in this climate and brought higher prices than chickens in the market.

"We have a flock of fifty," she said.

While Pete, Pam, Ricky, and Sue watched the lovely birds strutting around in the pen, Holly wandered off to the back of the property. She was surprised to see that it sloped down steeply to the shore of the river.

She turned to the others and called, "Pete! Pam! See how high this island sits up in the river!"

The others walked toward her in the snow as Holly leaned far over the edge of the embankment. Suddenly she gave a little cry as her feet slipped from under her.

"Holly! Holly!" Pam cried out, frightened.

She raced to help her sister, but Holly had already fallen over the edge of the snowy precipice and was out of sight!

CHAPTER 11

THE RIVERMEN

WITHOUT a moment's hesitation Pete slid down the embankment after Holly. Kicking up a shower of powdery snow, the boy went down the slope feet first.

Halfway down the precipice he found Holly clinging to a small tree. The boy dug his heels into the snow and grasped for a limb of the same tree. He made it!

"Hold on, Holly!" he encouraged his sister, who had hung over the out-jutting trunk like a sack of flour.

"I'm—I'm all right, Pete," Holly replied. "You'd better hang on or you'll fall to the bottom."

As Pete glanced down the steep slope to the snow-covered rocks beneath, he caught his breath. If he and Holly should fall any farther they might be badly hurt.

"What'll we do?" Holly asked in a small voice.

Both children looked up the cliff. Pete could see

at once that there was no possible way of their getting back except being dragged up by a rope. He himself might risk a slide to the bottom, but he would not want his sister to try it.

While he was pondering this, Holly spied a boat far out in the river. "Pete, some men are coming this way."

Turning his head, the boy saw an open boat with four men at oars and a fifth steering with a paddle. The craft was making its way through the freezing ice floes.

"Help! Help!" Pete shouted, hoping to attract their attention. But the men were too far away to hear his cries.

Holly now wriggled into a position where she could straddle the stout tree trunk. Then she took off her cap and waved it wildly.

The boat, the children noted, was headed for a small dock almost directly beneath them. Before long Holly's waving and Pete's shouting attracted the attention of the paddler. Looking up, he waved. Then he spoke to the rowers, who shipped their oars and turned to peer up the side of the cliff.

"Thank goodness they've seen us," Pete said, pulling himself up beside Holly.

The men leaned to their oars again, and soon the boat was alongside the dock. With a show of amazing strength, the five men pulled the boat up onto the wharf and turned it bottom-up.

Pete grinned. "If they're that strong, they should be able to rescue us," he said. Cupping his hands to his mouth, he hallooed to them, "Can you help us?"

The men shouted back in French, but from their gestures Pete understood that they were saying, "Hold on tightly!"

The steersman raced to a small hut not far from the dock and emerged carrying a coil of rope. The tallest and huskiest of the five men coiled it in his hand, then, stepping back, swung his arm in an arc and hurled the rope toward Pete. The end of it missed the boy's legs by inches and fell back.

"Oh dear!" said Holly.

The man coiled the rope again. Now Pete could see the muscles in the fellow's neck strain as he threw the coil with all his might. It snaked up the side of the cliff like a striking serpent. As it did, Pete leaned far out and caught the rope.

"*Bon! Bon!*" the men below shouted.

Pete could not understand their babble in French but he knew what to do. Pulling up the rope a few feet, he knotted the end about the tree trunk.

"We'll slide down, Holly," he said. "I'll go first and you follow me. But hold on tightly."

This was much to tom-boy Holly's liking. What

had started as an alarming accident now was turning out to be an exciting adventure.

Hand over hand Pete inched his way down the rope. A few feet from the ground he dropped off. "Oh, thanks for saving us," he said to the men. "*Merci.*" Then he looked up at Holly.

"Ready?" Pete asked.

"Okay," Holly said as she grasped the rope and swung her legs around it.

She slid down fast and fell into the outstretched arms of the rivermen.

"Thank you," said Holly. "You are such strong men."

The burly fellows grinned. Then for the first time the two children got a good look at them. The steersman, who was the shortest, smiled and doffed his red knitted cap. He wore a heavy gray turtle-neck sweater, corduroy trousers of the same color, and hip boots, as did the others.

The man bowed and said in halting English, "It is my pleasure to help you. I am Victor Tremblay and——"

"Tremblay!" Pete stared at the man as if he had seen a ghost.

"Ah, you have heard the name?"

"I'll say so!" Pete said. "You're the man we're looking for!"

He introduced himself and his sister. "We're part

Holly fell into the arms of the rivermen.

of the Hollister family you were sending a sleigh to," Pete said.

Victor's face brightened instantly. "You like it?" he said. "I think it is the best one I ever made."

The children looked at each other, perplexed. "We never got it," said Pete.

"What!" The sleigh maker began to wring his hands. "I have sent it to you. You should have received it for Christmas!"

Hardly believing what he heard, Victor Tremblay paced back and forth. "This is a terrible injustice to you Hollisters," he said. "I have been paid for the *cariole* and will give you your money back if we cannot find it."

"How did you send it to us?" Pete went on.

Victor Tremblay said that he had completed the sleigh on Ile aux Coudres. It had been carefully placed in a river craft and rowed to the other side, where it was entrusted to a man named Daniel Wilmot. He was to take it to Quebec where it would be shipped to the Hollisters.

"I think we should go and tell our family about this right away," said Pete. "They're up at the top of the cliff."

"Follow me," Victor directed and led the way to a small path which switched back and forth until it reached the top level of Ile aux Coudres.

On the way he said, "These men are my cousins,"

and introduced Laurent, Jean-Marc, Paul, and Marcel. One by one the men doffed their caps and bowed. Jean-Marc, the tallest of the four, was the one who had hurled the rope.

Pam, Ricky, and Sue, along with Gram, Gramp, and Tante Cecile ran through the snow to greet the rescued children and compliment the Tremblay men. After they had parked their boots outside the door of the house, everyone entered. Again the story of the *cariole* was told.

"You say a Daniel Wilmot actually sent it?" Gramp queried.

"He said he did," Victor replied. "And he is my friend. I cannot understand it."

Suddenly an alert look came into Pam's eyes. "Do you suppose it was sent to the wrong place?" she asked.

"I doubt it," Victor said, "because Mr. Wilmot had your address."

"Oh dear," Sue said. "We have to be detectives all over again."

The others smiled, then Victor Tremblay said with a sigh, "I wish you would be detectives to help us find my lost cousin Gabriel. I will explain. Another of my cousins, Gabriel, who is captain of our team for the annual canoe race, is missing."

"In the river?" Pam asked worriedly.

"No, he went to the Lake St. John country with a

friend to set traps. We have not heard from him, and, if he is not here for the canoe race, our boat cannot enter."

Gabriel, Victor went on to say, was the oldest of the cousins and the most experienced riverman. He and his four brothers had practiced for many months going across the river ice. They had a good chance to win the race, but without Gabriel there was no chance at all.

"That's too bad," Gram remarked.

"We'll find him!" Ricky said, jumping up. "But that means we'll have to stay here awhile and get some clues."

Tante Cecile smiled at the boy's enthusiasm. "We would be delighted if you would all spend the night with us," she said.

When Gram Hollister turned to her husband he spoke up, "That's very good of you. So much has happened since we arrived on the island that I'm afraid we've overstayed our time. I'm sure Mr. La Fontaine has left."

When it was agreed that the Hollisters would stay, the rivermen laughed and slapped their knees like happy children.

"Good!" Victor cried. "We do not see many people from the outside during the winter. We will be glad to have you."

"This is Gabriel," Jean-Marc said, picking up a

photograph from a table. "This picture was taken when he was making his traps."

The children gathered around to look at the picture. They saw a good-looking man with large brown eyes and a heavy brown beard. He was bent over an involved-looking arrangement of wood and steel.

"He looks as if he could find his way anywhere," Pam remarked admiringly. "Did he take a dog with him?"

"No," replied Laurent. "We haven't had a dog for some time."

"We have a dog," Sue piped up. "He's a collie, and his name is Zip."

"We have a donkey too," added Holly. "But just now he's lost."

The children all looked sad at the thought of the missing Domingo. To change the subject, Pete spoke up: "May we see your boat?"

"Of course," Victor replied.

So while Tante Cecile prepared supper the children joined Victor and retraced their steps down the long trail to the water front.

Because the canoe now lay on the dock the Hollisters could get a good look at it. Victor explained that it was twenty-two feet in length and was pointed at both ends. "That's what makes it a canoe," he said. "But I suppose in the United States you would call it a rowboat."

In answer to Ricky's questions, the children were told that the canoe was five feet two inches wide and weighed three hundred and eighty pounds. The craft was made of oak and cedar.

They could see a polished steel plate about a quarter of an inch thick which was used as the keel. "We slide the canoe over the ice on this keel," Victor went on.

It was an inch and a half at the front and increased in width until it was eight inches at the back.

"The three top planks are cedar," he said. "The others are oak to withstand the shock of the jagged ice."

"I'd like to take a ride in it," Ricky said, looking hopefully up at Victor.

"Not tonight. But tomorrow, perhaps."

As Victor started back up the trail with the girls, Pete and Ricky lingered behind. "We'd like to look at your canoe some more," Pete called. The others waved and disappeared up the slope.

After running his hand over the polished metal keel, Ricky said, "Boy, I'd like to be a riverman!"

"I would too!" his brother replied. "Say! Maybe we can practice right now."

"How?"

"Isn't that a little rowboat over there? Let's use it." He pointed to a small craft pulled up on the shore nearby.

The two boys pushed it into the icy river and jumped in.

"We won't go far," Pete said as he manned the oars.

Ricky climbed into the front and lay over the bow to push away several small ice floes which threatened to bump the craft.

"Isn't this neat!" he called.

Pete had not paid any attention to the current which began to push the small boat down the river with alarming speed. The boy pulled hard on the oars in an effort to get back to shore. But the floes closed in so fast that his oars could not reach over the ice into clear water.

A frightened look came into Pete's face. "Ricky, we're locked in the ice!"

CHAPTER 12

PAM'S MISHAP

"WHAT'LL we do now?" Ricky asked as the heavy river ice ground against the side of their tiny rowboat.

"We got ourselves into this," Pete said determinedly, "and we'll get ourselves out of it!"

He lifted the oars from the oarlocks and handed one to Ricky. "Here, push the ice away. I'll help you."

The boys strained and tugged, finally clearing a space around the boat. Pete quickly jumped back, replaced the oars, and rowed furiously. He managed to advance a few feet before the ice closed in. The same method was tried again and again. By poling, pushing, and rowing the Hollisters finally reached the shore.

They were out of breath and panted as they beached the boat, pulling it up on the pebbly riverbank. Then they started up the cliffside trail.

"Pete," said Ricky with a grin as they climbed the hill, "we're rivermen now!"

Pete reflected for a moment, then chuckled. "I guess we are, but just the same we'll be more careful next time."

Supper was ready when the boys reached the Tremblays' farmhouse. It was a simple meal of baked fish, boiled carrots, and stewed apples. How good it tasted to the Hollisters after their lively day!

"Our diet here is very limited," said Tante Cecile. "Living on the island, we have to depend on ourselves for food so we store everything but the fish. Would you like to see our root cellar where we keep some of it?"

"Oh yes."

After Pam and Holly had helped with the dishes and Pete had brought in more wood for the stove, Tante Cecile said, "Now I'll show you our root cellar."

For the first time the children noticed a trap door in the far left corner of the big room. Pierre Tremblay opened it, revealing a stairway leading down into a musty cavern. Holding a lantern, Tante Cecile led the way down, and the children followed.

In the root cellar were three enormous bins. One contained potatoes, another apples, and the third carrots with dirt thrown over the top of them.

"Outside of fish the men catch, this is our winter's main food supply," Tante Cecile said. She smiled. "We had a good apple crop this year." Then she added proudly, "My boys have the best orchard on the island!"

"I didn't know there were so many potatoes in the whole world!" Holly giggled. "Your boys must have big appetites."

"Indeed they do." The woman laughed.

"This is a nice place," said Sue, sniffing the fruity aroma. "I like it. Every time I wanted an apple I could just run down here and get one!" She went around the side of the bin for a better look.

When the children returned upstairs and the trap door was closed, Pam noticed that Sue was missing. "Where did she go?"

"Maybe she stayed in the cellar," Holly suggested, "to eat an apple."

The trap door was raised, and Pam called down, "Sue, are you there?"

"Yes, Pam, and I'm almost eaten."

Laughing and wondering what she meant, the others waited. In a moment Sue appeared holding the core of an apple, her eyes mischievous.

"Oh, you funny little girl," said Gram, chuckling. "I'm never sure what you mean."

It was soon time for Sue, Holly, and Ricky to go to bed, and Gram went upstairs with them. Cots for the Hollister family had been arranged in a row in the large open room on the second floor. There was a small partitioned area at one end which served as a place in which to dress and undress.

While the Tremblay brothers, Victor, and Gramp played cards at the large table downstairs, Pam and Pete sat on the floor before the fire. In whispered conversation they discussed the various mysteries in which they were involved—their missing Domingo, the lost *cariole,* and now the disappearance of Gabriel Tremblay.

"I sure hope our burro's been found," said Pete. "We probably won't know though, until Dad and Mother get here."

"Yes," Pam agreed. "Poor Domingo! If he's left out in the cold, he'll get sick."

Pete nodded, then said, "Pam, as soon as we get back to Quebec, I'm going to work real hard to find our *cariole.* I have a hunch it never left Quebec!"

"You could be right. Say, Pete," his sister said suddenly, jumping up, "I have an idea."

"About what?"

"Gabriel Tremblay. You remember the short-wave set Mr. La Fontaine has? Why couldn't he help us?"

Pete jumped up too. "Sure, Sis. He could contact other hams around the area where Gabriel went. He might get some news!"

The two children were so excited by the idea that they rushed across the room to the dining table. They waited for the cardplayers to finish a hand, then Pete told them the plan.

"That is a very good thought, very good," said

Victor. "Now why didn't one of us think of it?" He smiled. "I can see why you children are called young detectives."

Pete and Pam flushed a little, and Pam said, "Mr. La Fontaine won't be here until tomorrow afternoon. Oh, I wish we could ask him sooner!"

"Maybe you can," Victor told them. "Early to-morrow morning my cousins and I are taking the canoe to Baie St. Paul."

"And you mean we might go with you?" Pam asked eagerly.

Victor smiled. "We had better wait until morning before deciding," he said. "The river can be very tricky."

The next day the Hollisters awakened to beautiful, clear weather and the delightful aroma of breakfast being prepared on the wood stove. As they ate hot cereal sprinkled with brown sugar, Victor addressed the children.

"My cousins and I will definitely row across the river to Baie St. Paul this morning. We can take two passengers."

All the children wanted to go, but Gram felt it would be best for the two boys to accompany the men on the rugged trip.

Tante Cecile, seeing the disappointment on the faces of the girls, said, "Don't worry, we'll find lots to do here. You can help me make apple-tree markers to begin with."

"That sounds like fun," Holly said. "How do we do it?"

"I'll show you presently," the Canadian woman answered with a smile.

The rivermen donned their heavy sweaters and caps, then pulled on their rubber boots. The Hollister brothers quickly put on their own heavy coats, caps, and boots.

"Come on, boys," Victor said, and Pete and Ricky waved good-by to their family.

They followed the path down to the river front, and the Tremblays launched their canoe. While Pete and Ricky hopped into the front, the four Canadian brothers took their places at the oars. Victor shoved off from the dock with a paddle. Powerful strokes sped the canoe across small channels of water amid the ice floes.

Back in the farmhouse, meanwhile, Pam, Holly, and Sue were busy learning to make apple-tree markers. Tante Cecile had taken two old window shades from a closet.

"You use these?" Holly asked.

"Yes, dear." To the amazement of Gram, Gramp, and the three girls, Tante Cecile ripped a long strip from the edge of one of the shades up to the roller. Then with nimble fingers she went *rip, rip, rip,* until the entire shade was a series of one-inch strips.

Seeing it, Sue chuckled. "This looks like a hula skirt," she said, giggling.

Tante Cecile laughed. "I never thought of that." She supplied the girls with scissors and told them to cut each strip into ten-inch pieces. The children went to work, carefully snipping the long strips into the proper length.

"Each of these pieces," said Tante Cecile, "will be marked with the variety of the young tree to which it will be attached and then wrapped around the slender trunk. We'll have a thousand of these strips," she continued, "because we'll have that many new apple trees in the orchard this year."

"Are we going to make all those now?" Holly asked.

"Ah no. Only what we get from these two shades."

It did not take long for the visitors to finish their job. When the two shades had been cut up, Tante Cecile asked, "Would you girls like to look in my costume trunk?"

"Oh yes!" said Sue excitedly.

The girls followed Tante Cecile upstairs to where an old trunk stood in one corner of the big room. When opened, it proved to be filled with children's old-fashioned clothes. The French-Canadian woman took out a few dresses and handed them to the girls.

"Oh, how cute and frilly!" Pam said as she held up a green-and-white-striped, lace-trimmed dress which reached from her shoulders to the floor.

"This long blue one with the great big sleeves should fit me," Holly said. "May I try it on?"

"What are these funny long pants?"

"Yes."

"I like this one," Sue remarked, "but what are these funny long white pants?"

"Pantaloons, my dear. They will look very cute on you with this full pink dress and bonnet."

The girls quickly put on the costumes, pirouetting and dancing around the room in the old-fashioned frocks.

"And look at this," said Tante Cecile, holding up a tiny red hat.

"Goodness!" Holly said. "That's not for a child, is it?"

Tante Cecile said no, it had belonged to a monkey. Her grandfather, sailing home from Africa, had brought a pet monkey with him. The hat had been made for the little animal many, many years before.

"I know who could wear it right now," Sue declared. "Mr. Mailloux's dog."

"*Poilu?*"

"Yes, it would fit him fine."

"Then why not take it to him?" Tante Cecile suggested, smiling.

"Oh, we'd love to," Pam declared and Holly added, "He needs one 'cause he's always taking his master's hat."

The three girls took off their costumes and donned boots and coats for the walk to Mr. Mailloux's place. Pam tucked the little hat in her pocket.

Running and skipping along the snowy roadside the girls reached Mr. Mailloux's quaint farmhouse and knocked on the door. "Come in, come in," the kindly man said. "I suppose you want to play with *Poilu?*"

"Yes," Pam said as she unbuttoned her coat. "And we have a little gift for him."

Just then *Poilu* came bounding into the room. Pam called him. When he ran up to her, she put the tiny hat on his head. An elastic under his chin held it in place. The little dog cocked his head one way, then another, seemingly very proud of his new *chapeau*.

"Now I'll take off *your* hat," Holly said, leaning down.

But *Poilu* was too quick for her. He darted off, tilting the hat so it covered his left eye. None of the girls could catch him.

"You're an old tease," said Holly.

After the three sisters had played with *Poilu* for a while Pam said, "I think we should go back to the Tremblays' now. Maybe Mr. La Fontaine will come with some news."

As the girls opened the front door, *Poilu*, still wearing his red hat, ran out.

"Come back," Holly ordered.

Mr. Mailloux too called his little pet, but the dog paid no attention. Instead, he followed the girls when they left. Reaching the road, Pam turned and said sternly, "Go home, *Poilu*. Your master wants you."

Poilu merely wagged his tail and continued to follow them.

"I know why he won't go back," Sue declared. "He doesn't understand English!"

"That's right," Pam said. "I guess I'd better pick him up and carry him back."

But as she leaned down *Poilu* dashed into a nearby field. Pam ran after him. *Poilu* leaped over what seemed to be a small ditch. As Pam tried to follow she suddenly slipped down through the snow.

"Oh!" she cried out, and would have disappeared entirely if she had not grasped the edge of a brick-lined hole. "Help! Help!"

Her sisters ran to Pam, whose fingers were slipping from the ledge. "I'm in a well but I can't touch bottom," she wailed. "Get somebody! Quick!"

Instead, Holly and Sue tugged at Pam's wrists, trying to lift her from the abandoned well, all the while shouting for help. They did not succeed in pulling Pam out. And at any moment she might slip from their grip. Adding to the confusion was *Poilu*, who ran around in circles and barked loudly.

"Oh, if Mr. Mailloux would only hear us!" Holly said tearfully. "Help! Help!"

CHAPTER 13

DISHEARTENING NEWS

"HOLD on, Pam!" Holly begged as one of her sister's hands slipped off the edge of the wellhole. Pam dug into a little opening with the toe of her boot and for the moment kept from falling.

"Help! Help!" Sue shouted with all her might.

Suddenly the door of Mr. Mailloux's house sprang open, and the old farmer came running toward them. Reaching the abandoned well, he bent down with Sue and Holly, and together they pulled Pam out.

For a few minutes the girl sat on the ground, weak from her struggles. Panting, she whispered, "Oh, thank you!"

"My dear," Mr. Mailloux said as he lifted his cap to mop his brow, "if you had fallen to the bottom you might have broken a leg."

In a few moments Pam's strength was restored, and she rose to her feet. Holly and Sue brushed the snow from their sister's coat.

The islander patted Pam's shoulder. "Come back

to my house and rest a while before you go home."

It seemed to the three girls as if *Poilu* sensed that his mischief had led them into trouble. The little dog came up to Pam and whimpered. She set his red hat on straight, after which he followed them obediently to the house. Mr. Mailloux prepared three cups of steaming hot cider and served it with cookies.

"Yum, this is good," said Pam.

The girls had nearly finished the treat when there was a knock on the door. When Mr. Mailloux opened it, they saw Gram and Gramp standing there.

"We thought you girls were lost!" Gram said with a chuckle.

"We nearly were—in a big hole," Sue remarked, and told what had happened.

Gramp shook his head and said to Mr. Mailloux, "Keeping up with our grandchildren's adventures is a full-time job. They seem to get into one difficulty after another."

"But they always come out all right," Holly boasted.

After Gram and Gramp had cups of hot cider also, the Hollisters bid Mr. Mailloux good-by and trudged back along the snowy road.

"I wonder if Pete and Ricky are at Mr. La Fontaine's yet," Pam mused as she followed Gramp's boot prints.

The brothers had had an exciting morning too.

When the Tremblays' canoe was halfway across the river, Jean-Marc noticed an eager look in the faces of their visitors. He spoke rapidly to Victor in French. The sleigh maker replied with a smile, "I think that would be all right. How would you boys like to help us?"

"Crickets!" Pete exclaimed. "You mean rowing?"

Victor said that Pete might spell Jean-Marc at one of the oars while Ricky could steer. Quickly the boys changed places with the men. The Tremblay brothers rowed slower so that Pete could keep up with the stroke.

Ricky's face wore an ear-to-ear grin as he grasped the long paddle and guided the craft in and out of the ice floes. "I'm glad I had that practice yesterday," he thought.

Victor told the Hollisters how the tide had proved to be a problem for the rivermen. "We can't go straight across the St. Lawrence," he explained. "The current and the tide make us move up or down stream, so we have to start at a point above or below where we intend to land. That is why we had to set out at a certain time this morning."

Pete and Ricky could see what was happening. They had started out some distance below Baie St. Paul. Now, with the incoming tide pushing the river backwards, they seemed to be making their way directly toward a dock near the Hotel Eau Claire.

"Perfect timing!" Pete said admiringly when the boat pulled alongside.

They all hopped out and the rivermen turned their craft over on the dock to protect it from the ice.

"We shall go to the post office first," Victor said. "It is my cousins' job to pick up the island's mail."

Hearing this, Pete asked, "Do you mind if Rick and I go straight to the La Fontaines'? I want to ask the pilot about trying to find Gabriel."

"By all means," Victor answered. "We'll be there in a little while."

Pete and Ricky dashed toward the hotel, eager to talk to its owner. They found Jacques trying out a pair of small skis on the landing strip.

"Hi!" Ricky cried out, running up to him. "How are you today?"

"*Bien! Bien!*" the rosy-cheeked boy replied. "I am waiting for *mon père*," the boy said, pointing skyward. He told the Hollisters that his father had flown two hunters into the interior that morning but was due to return shortly.

"We want to see him," said Pete. "We'll wait. Jacques, do you want to be a pilot someday too?"

"*Oui*," the boy replied. "I am practicing now. See?" With that he unbuttoned his coat and held it outstretched like a bird's wings. The strong wind, whipping across the landing strip, carried him over the hard-packed snow.

"That's a good landing, Jacques," Pete said, running along beside the skiing boy.

Ricky begged to try it, so Jacques removed his skis, and Ricky fitted them to his feet. He held his coat open. *Whiz!* He shot across the runway.

Just then the sound of the airplane's motor attracted their attention. They glanced up to see the red speck of Mr. La Fontaine's craft growing larger and larger as it headed for the airfield.

The plane circled over the place once, dipping its wings as Jacques' father recognized the lads beneath him. Then it came around for a landing. Just as the skis were about to touch the runway, a strong gust blew an empty gasoline drum onto its side and rolled it over the air strip.

The drum was directly in the path of Mr. La Fontaine's taxiing plane!

"Pete! He's going to crash into the can!" Ricky cried.

His brother had already seen the predicament and was dashing across the strip. Reaching the empty gasoline drum, he gave it a hard push, sending it out of the path of the onrushing plane. Then Pete flattened himself on the runway and the plane passed by him, coming to a stop near the back of the farmhouse restaurant.

Mr. La Fontaine hopped out, bent down to hug his son, then shook Pete's hand. "You are a brave boy to

Pete gave the gasoline drum a hard push.

do that," he said. "The only chance I had was to take off again, but I don't know whether I could have made it or not."

The pilot put the gasoline drum in a nearby shed where it could do no more harm.

"We'd like to talk to you," said Pete.

"Come right in." Mr. La Fontaine smiled.

Following the pilot, the boys entered the back door of the restaurant and found themselves in a large kitchen. A corner of it was used for the family's dining. Mrs. La Fontaine greeted them all and at once served cups of steaming hot chocolate. As they drank it, Pete told about the missing Gabriel Tremblay, who was presumably in the Lake St. John country.

"Ah yes," the pilot said. "I know that area well. It is easy to get lost up there."

"Mr. La Fontaine," Pete said, leaning forward, "do you think you might use your short-wave radio to try finding out about him?"

"Yes, I believe I could," the pilot replied.

At that moment footsteps sounded at the rear door, and the Tremblay cousins, along with Victor, entered the restaurant kitchen. The La Fontaines at once expressed their concern over Gabriel's absence.

"*C'est dommage*," said the pilot's wife. "That's a pity," she translated for the Hollisters.

But Mr. La Fontaine smiled. "Pete has given me an idea. Maybe I can help you. I have a friend at

Lake St. John who is a ham too and can pick up my short-wave radio signals." He rose from his chair and beckoned to the three boys. "Come with me."

Pete, Ricky, and Jacques followed Mr. La Fontaine up the two flights of steps to his small attic room. At once the pilot sat down at his table which held all the equipment. The Hollister boys listened open-mouthed as the French Canadian spoke hastily in his native language. Finally a voice replied over the loud-speaker, and a rapid conversation ensued. Then Mr. La Fontaine said, "*Merci, merci,*" and signed off.

"What did he say?" Ricky asked as Mr. La Fontaine headed for the stairs.

"The news isn't good," the pilot replied.

When he reached the kitchen, Mr. La Fontaine explained that there had been a severe blizzard in the Lake St. John area. Gabriel had probably been out in it and no doubt had headed for the nearest shelter.

"He may be holed up there for a long time," the pilot added.

Hearing this, the rivermen looked both relieved and discouraged. They were happy to learn that Gabriel was only snowbound and not a victim of the blizzard. But Victor expressed their disappointment. Rising from his chair, he gave a great sigh.

"Now we will not be able to enter the ice-canoe race at Quebec!" he said forlornly.

CHAPTER 14

SNOWBOUND HUNTERS

THE disconsolate looks on the faces of the Tremblays made Pete and Ricky sad. The Hollisters, in solving other mysteries, had always managed to help people in need. Now the two boys had the same thought in mind. What else could they do to find Gabriel, so that the Tremblay canoe could be entered in the Quebec race?

Suddenly Pete had an idea. His eyes brightened as he addressed Mr. La Fontaine. "Could Ricky and I hunt for Gabriel with you in your plane?"

The pilot was hesitant to reply. But Jacques spoke up. "*Mon père* can find Gabriel Tremblay. I know it!"

This caused his father to smile. He drew in a deep breath and exhaled slowly. "It is an almost impossible task to find one man in the wilderness," he said.

"But there's always a chance you can," Pete urged.

"You're right."

"Then let's take it," Pete said eagerly.

"But your grandparents——" the pilot went on. "Maybe they would not like you to do such a thing."

"I'm sure Gram and Gramp would let us go," Pete said hopefully. "The Tremblays have been wonderful to us and if we can repay them in some way——"

"All right, I'll do it if you get your grandparents' consent."

It was decided that the boys would return to Ile aux Coudres by canoe and get the permission. Mr. La Fontaine would devote the rest of the day to tuning up his airplane motor and preparing for the trip. "We will start early tomorrow morning," he said. "I will pick you up."

The pilot promised to study his aerial maps that night and also wireless to his friend at Lake St. John to learn if there was further information about Gabriel.

The trip back across the river was made in record time. Pete was the first to burst into the Tremblay farmhouse with news of their latest adventure. "Please, may we go?" he begged after telling their story.

"Won't it be dangerous?" Gram asked cautiously.

"You know Mr. La Fontaine is a wonderful pilot," Pete said. "Besides, with the skis on his plane he can land almost anywhere in the north country."

"There are a lot of frozen lakes," Gramp put in. "Still——"

"Oh, please let them go," Pam pleaded.

Gramp Hollister stroked his chin thoughtfully. Finally he said, "It's all right with me if it is with your grandmother."

"I'll consent," came her answer at last. "I have a feeling everything will be fine. You may go."

"Yippee!" the boys exclaimed.

Instantly the Happy Hollister children began dancing around joyfully. Tante Cecile smiled and the rugged rivermen beamed with admiration for the plucky children.

"*Bonne chance! Bonne chance!*" Victor said as he shook the hands of Pete and Ricky.

"Does that mean good luck?" Pam asked him.

"*Oui,*" Jean-Marc spoke up. "We will pray for you!"

Next morning, before sunup, Tante Cecile roused the boys. After breakfast the snowmobile came for Pete and Ricky and took them to the airfield. Mr. La Fontaine was waiting, the engine of his plane idling.

"*Bon jour*, fellows," he said. "Hop in."

The Hollister boys stepped aboard. Now the engine roared, and the plane sped down the strip. Its nose lifted. The snowy runway dropped away below them, and the search was on!

Once they had gained the proper altitude, Mr. La Fontaine said, "We have good news to start our trip."

"What is it?" Pete asked eagerly.

"I contacted my friend at Lake St. John again and learned that Gabriel and his companion set their traps near Frog Lake. They became separated in the blizzard. Gabriel's friend returned safely, and now woodsmen are organizing a search party."

Ricky's eyes glistened. "Maybe we can find him first!"

"Perhaps," the pilot said. He laid a map on the knees of Pete, who sat beside him. "Here's Frog Lake," he pointed out. "We will get there in about an hour."

The plane had left the course of the St. Lawrence River and was flying over snow-draped forests which clothed the hilly ridges. Occasionally a group of skiers could be seen far below, appearing like tiny ants as they glided down the slopes.

Finally a broad frozen expanse appeared on the horizon. "That's Lake St. John," Mr. La Fontaine said. "Frog Lake is beyond."

It took several minutes to fly across Lake St. John. Once on the other side, the pilot dipped the plane lower. "Do you see a white spot shaped like a bullfrog? That will be Frog Lake," he told his passengers.

Ricky pressed close to the window, and Pete peered straight ahead but the boys could see only an endless stretch of forest.

Finally, however, Ricky cried out, "I think I see it!"

"Where?" Pete asked.

"Over there on the left behind that ridge."

The pilot banked and flew over the spot. "That's it," he said.

The small, snow-covered lake, outlined with dark trees, looked like a bullfrog in the middle of a leap.

The pilot cut his motor, and the plane glided lower and lower. "We'll land on the lake," he said.

The aircraft cleared a tall stand of pines and began settling rapidly.

"Look!" Pete exclaimed, pointing to his right. "A cabin! There's smoke coming from the chimney!"

"Maybe Gabriel's there!" Ricky exclaimed as the plane's skis touched down and slid over the snow.

The pilot turned off the engine, and the plane stopped. Then he instructed Ricky to open the small door of the baggage compartment. "You'll find snow-shoes in there," he said. "We'll need them."

Ricky reached for the bulky snowshoes. He passed them forward to Pete, who threw them out on the snow. All hopped down and adjusted the webbed shoes onto their boots.

"I feel like a duck!" Ricky exclaimed, lifting his

They plowed ahead toward the lonesome cabin.

feet high as they plowed ahead toward the lonesome cabin.

It was a small building made of logs, with a door and one window which was nearly concealed by a snowdrift.

"I don't see any footprints," Mr. La Fontaine said as they came closer. "Whoever's in here has been holed up for several days."

Just then Ricky glanced toward the back of the cabin and gave an involuntary cry.

"What's the matter?" Pete asked.

"A big animal is back there! I saw it move!"

Mr. La Fontaine led the way to the rear of the hut. There stood a gigantic bull moose. He seemed just as surprised as the three searchers.

"Crickets!" Pete exclaimed. "The size of that animal!"

"Will he hurt us?" Ricky whispered.

As if in reply, the bull moose turned quickly in its tracks and with an ungainly lope dashed for the shelter of the forest.

"Once in a while you find a curious moose, although in the main they are shy," Mr. La Fontaine said as they made their way to the cabin door.

Pete knocked on it. There was no reply. He knocked again.

"Who's there?" came a muffled voice from inside.

"Is that you, Gabriel?" the pilot cried.

The door opened a crack, and a heavily bearded man peered out at them. Then he opened the door wide. "Come in," he said. "My name's not Gabriel. I'm John Thompson."

After Pete, Ricky, and Mr. La Fontaine had introduced themselves, Ricky asked, "Do you live out here in the woods alone all the time, Mr. Thompson?"

"I guess I'm what you call an old codger," he said, smiling. "I love to hunt and live alone. Sort of like a hermit, you know."

The hunter said that his home was in Winnipeg, but that each winter he came to the cabin to spend several months in the wilds. On further questioning, Mr. Thompson said that he had not seen Gabriel Tremblay.

"But," said Mr. Thompson, "if he's in this area there's one shelter he might have found—a tiny cabin twenty-five miles to the north on a small lake called Marie's Diamond."

"*Oui, oui,*" said the pilot quickly.

As they chatted, Mr. Thompson made his visitors a drink from bouillon cubes and hot melted snow. "I wish you luck," he said as they started off on their search.

After climbing into the plane after the boys, Mr. La Fontaine took off and headed for the small lake known as Marie's Diamond. It was called this, the pilot said, because it glittered brilliantly in the summer sunshine.

He had no trouble finding the lake, but landing was another problem. Mr. La Fontaine circled the area several times, looking for a suitable spot to come down on the ice.

Finally he brought the plane very low. It seemed to Pete as if the topmost branches of the trees must brush against the fuselage. But the pilot dropped the nose sharply, then brought it up and landed perfectly.

"*Aie!*" he said. "I wouldn't like to do that many times."

How skillful he was, Pete thought!

"There's the cabin," Ricky said, and pointed toward a grove of trees near the shore. Among them nestled a hut.

Donning their snowshoes again, the three hastened to the tiny structure which looked no larger than a lean-to. Its small door was covered by a tarpaulin.

"Anybody home?" Pete cried out hopefully as he plodded up to it.

CHAPTER 15

DISCOVERED

SUDDENLY a huge man stood framed in the doorway of the forest hut. His powerful voice had a cheerful ring as he shouted:

"*La Fontaine! Mon bon ami!*"

"Gabriel!"

The two men advanced toward each other and embraced in French fashion—a bear hug with a touching of cheeks, first one then the other. After a rapid conversation, accompanied by many gestures of the hands and loud laughter, the pilot suddenly stopped and said to the children, "Pete, Ricky, forgive me. You do not understand French."

"Is this really Gabriel Tremblay?" Ricky asked.

"Indeed it is." The pilot introduced the boys, and they all went inside.

The cabin was crudely furnished. A large bearskin rug lay on the earthen floor. On a rough log table lay a woodsman's skillet and fork, and there was a gasoline cooking stove at the end. A single bunk with a sleeping bag was built against one wall.

The men sat down on the bunk, the boys on the floor. Mr. La Fontaine translated Gabriel's story. He had wandered through the storm to the hut and had conserved his energy until he was to start the long trek back home that afternoon.

"But he wouldn't have got back in time for the Quebec race," Pete said, then grinned. "But now he will!"

"*Merci, merci!*" Gabriel cried out gratefully when he was told what the boy had said.

After the riverman had gathered his gear, the group set off and boarded the plane. The take-off was smooth and expert. Soon they were winging over the forests on a bee line for Ile aux Coudres.

By the time Mr. La Fontaine had circled for a landing, a group of people, including the Hollisters, had gathered alongside the cornfield runway. When the propeller stopped whirling, they swooped on the plane. Seeing Gabriel jump down, they gave loud cries of joy.

"Oh, look!" Sue said as she watched the scene. "Everybody is hugging everybody!"

"An old French custom," her grandfather answered.

When the native onlookers heard that the Hollisters —Pete in particular—were responsible for setting in motion the wheels which started the successful search for Gabriel, they broke into cheers. Then each of the Hollisters received a French-style hug from the Tremblays.

"Oo, Quebecland is nice," said Sue, who had received her special hug from Tante Cecile.

The woman smiled, then said she was very grateful for what the Happy Hollisters had done. "As a gift I want you to take home some of the old French costumes you girls saw. And there are two suits that will fit the boys. You may like to use them in a play sometime."

Ricky grinned. "*Merci! S'il vous plaît*, and everything else."

The other children thanked her, then got into the snowmobile. When they reached the Tremblay house, Gramp asked the driver to wait.

Turning to the Tremblays he said, "I think we Hollisters should leave at once and go back to Quebec. Mr. La Fontaine is waiting for us."

"We're sorry to see you go," said Tante Cecile. "I'll get the costumes." She hurried to get them while Pete and Ricky went for the overnight bags.

As the group gathered to say good-by, Victor said, "I hope you find the *cariole*. If you do not, let me know. I will build you another." Then he added, "You will watch the race, of course."

"We'll all be there," Pete promised.

After fond good-bys the Hollisters left and a little while later landed at the La Fontaines' hotel. Here they climbed into their sedan and rode to Quebec. It was nearly dark by the time they arrived at their hotel.

No sooner had they removed their wraps than Pam said to her grandparents, "I'd like to telephone the police station. Maybe they'll know what happened to our *cariole*."

"Go ahead."

Connected with headquarters, Pam's call was given to an English-speaking sergeant. After hearing about the mystery, the officer said that they had heard nothing of a missing *cariole* with the initials "H.H."

"But I'll put men on the lookout," he offered.

"*Merci*," Pam said as she hung up.

"I want to telephone too," Sue said after her sister had put down the receiver. "But my call's to Mommy and Daddy."

"Good idea!" Pete said. "Maybe they've found Domingo."

"And I want to know when they're coming here," Gramp remarked. "Who wants to put in the call?"

"I will," Pete volunteered.

It did not take long for the call to be put through to Shoreham.

"Hello, Mother!" Pete cried out as Mrs. Hollister answered on the other end.

"Why, hello, dear. You sound so close!" she said.

What excited conversation followed! Each of the children, as well as Gram and Gramp, was given a chance to say hello. Mr. and Mrs. Hollister reported that they would arrive in Quebec by plane on Sunday.

Domingo had not yet been found, but some small children had seen the burro in a field on the other side of town. The police, however, had been unable to locate the missing pet.

"But it's only Friday," said Mrs. Hollister. "They still have another day to search for him before Dad and I leave. Maybe we'll bring you good news."

Long after the phone call was over the children chatted about their missing pet. "If Domingo has been seen, I'm sure he'll be found by Officer Cal," Pam said hopefully.

"And then if we find our *cariole*," Holly exclaimed, "all the mysteries will be solved."

Just then the phone rang. Gram Hollister answered it. "Yes, yes. That will be fine. *Merci*," she said, and hung up.

"What is it, Gram?" Pete asked eagerly.

"The hotel hostess says there will be a masquerade party tonight at the Coliseum and she would like us to attend."

"In costume?" Holly asked.

"Yes. It's fortunate Tante Cecile gave you the old French outfits."

After supper the Hollister children dressed in their

old-time French-Canadian costumes. Pete and Ricky grinned at themselves in the mirror.

"I feel silly," said Ricky, eyeing his tight maroon velvet pants and gold-braided short jacket.

"Me too," Pete added. He wore a similar black velvet costume with long white stockings.

"You're a beautiful-looking family," Gram beamed. "Well, we'd better go."

The outside temperature hovered around zero as Gramp drove to the Coliseum. It was a huge, domed building, surrounded by acres of parking area in which there were hundreds of cars. Gramp found a space and drove in.

The children ran on ahead into the brightly lighted building. Immediately music greeted their ears.

"Oh, isn't this wonderful?" said Pam.

Gramp bought tickets in the corridor, and the whole family walked up a ramp which led to the center of the Coliseum. The children gasped in amazement at the sight before them. Tiers of seats for spectators banked the huge floor of polished wood where hundreds of people in all kinds of costumes danced gaily. A band at the south end of the floor was playing a lively tune.

"Look at the funny costumes!" Ricky exclaimed.

Glancing at the dancers nearby, the boy could see monkeys, Zulus, French cavaliers, Indians, football players, a butterfly, and a ballerina.

"I've never seen so many different costumes before," Gram agreed. "Some are gorgeous."

Gram and Gramp remained in the stands while the children walked onto the floor. The boys took turns dancing with their sisters. When Ricky twirled little Sue about, the onlookers clapped.

A man with a pad and pencil, walking among the revelers, stopped and said to Pam, "Do you children all belong to one family?" he asked.

"Yes we do. We're the Happy Hollisters from Shoreham in the States."

"Welcome to Quebec!" The man smiled. "I hope you have a very good time here." He walked on.

The dancing continued for more than an hour. When the music stopped, a handsome man in evening clothes spoke through the band's loud-speaker in French.

"Oh, I wish I knew what he was saying," Pam remarked.

Hearing this, a beautiful young woman who stood nearby in the costume of a French doll smiled. "I will translate for you," she said kindly. "They will now judge costumes. There are many classifications for prizes."

Pam looked admiringly at their translator and wondered whether her French-doll costume might win a prize.

"I am Marielle Dumas," said the young woman, "and I am one of the seven duchesses."

After the Hollister children had introduced themselves, Pam asked what a duchess was. Marielle explained that seven duchesses were chosen from the seven districts of Quebec. One of them would be the Carnival queen and the six others would be her attendants.

"How lovely!" said Pam, and Holly remarked, "Then you're famous, aren't you?"

Marielle laughed gaily at this remark. She said it was great fun to be a duchess. In the big carnival parade they would ride in *carioles* preceding the queen.

Marielle stayed with the five Hollisters while the judging of the costumes proceeded. A young man dressed in a giraffe's suit took the prize as the most original. The award for the funniest went to a clown with a cabbage head.

Suddenly the Hollisters heard Marielle Dumas's name called out. Her costume was chosen as the most beautiful.

"Hurray! Hurray!" Sue cried out, and the other Hollisters complimented her.

The announcer spoke again, and Marielle translated for the children. "Now comes the prize for the best family group. Look, one of the judges is coming your way!"

The Hollisters stood openmouthed as a young man

wearing silk breeches, a jacket with lace at the sleeves, and a white wig, beckoned them forward. In the clapping and confusion the children hardly knew what was happening. They were ushered up onto the musicians' stage, Marielle behind them. Then the loudspeaker boomed forth again.

"You have won a prize," Marielle whispered, "for the family group wearing authentic period costumes."

The Hollisters had never been more surprised. Pam and her sisters curtsied while Pete and Ricky bowed to the cheering crowd. Each of the children was given a golden medallion as a memento of the event.

"This is so much fun!" Holly declared as they returned to the huge dance floor and walked to where Gram and Gramp were waiting.

"Congratulations to our wonderful grandchildren!" Gram said gaily.

Marielle, who had accompanied them, was introduced. Then she asked what had brought the Hollisters to Quebec. Pete related the story of the missing *cariole*.

"We're having trouble finding it," he added, and said that their sleuthing was doubly difficult in Quebec because they did not speak French.

"Oh, don't worry about that," Marielle said. "I will help you. How would you like me to be your interpreter? I have tomorrow free."

"Here, Sue," the Duchess said, "sit on my lap."

Her offer was accepted immediately by the enthusiastic children.

"I can meet you at your hotel at ten tomorrow morning," Marielle said.

"Great!" Pete declared. "With you helping us, I'm certain we'll find our sleigh."

Marielle bent down to kiss little Sue, then said goodby and disappeared onto the dance floor. Soon afterward the Hollisters left. Half an hour later the five children were asleep, weary from a day of excitement and full of hope for their sleuthing the next day.

At ten o'clock sharp Marielle met them in the lobby of the hotel. "Where do we go first?" she asked, laughing.

Pete suggested that they go to the freight station to see whether or not the *cariole* had reached there.

"Then I have a suggestion," Marielle said. "How would you all like to ride there in my family's sleigh? It's large enough for all of us."

"Goody, goody!" exclaimed Sue. "May I drive the horse?"

"Of course," Marielle said. She led the children to the street, where a glistening red and white sleigh stood at the curb. Hitched to it was a dappled horse. He pawed at the snow impatiently.

Pete, Ricky, and Holly climbed into the back seat while Pam and Sue took places in front beside Marielle.

"Here, Sue," the duchess said, taking the reins, "sit in my lap."

Their knees covered by two bearskin robes, the children shouted they were ready to go. Marielle gave the horse a light slap with the reins, and off they went, up one street and down another until they descended a steep hill to the railroad station.

"The freight office is inside," Marielle said.

"I'll inquire about the *cariole*," Pete volunteered.

Entering the building, he made his way to the freight window. Fortunately the clerk on duty spoke both English and French.

After Pete had told his story the man said, "Come to think of it, yes, I do remember that we shipped a *cariole*—but it came back."

Pete looked startled. "Why was that?"

The clerk thumbed through a sheaf of papers, finally pulling one out and showing it to Pete. "Here," he said, "this may explain it."

CHAPTER 16

HOT ON THE TRAIL

THE freight agent, who said his name was Henri, handed the shipping order to Pete, who glanced at it quickly. The name of the sender was correct—Victor Tremblay. Now suddenly part of the mystery unfolded as Pete read on.

"Sent to John Hollister, Shoreham, California."

"California!" Pete called out. "That's not our state!"

"Then there's the mistake," the freight man said. "That's why the *cariole* was returned to Quebec."

"But why wasn't Victor Tremblay told about this?" Pete inquired.

The clerk said he had tried to locate the sleigh maker without success. After Pete told briefly of their adventure on Ile aux Coudres, the freight man congratulated him on the Hollisters' fine sleuthing.

"You've found Tremblay, and now about your *cariole*——"

"Yes, where is it?" Pete queried anxiously, half trembling with excitement.

"In our warehouse."

"May we get it right away?"

Henri said that the place was closed on Saturday.

"Crickets!" Pete declared in disappointment. "You mean we can't get our *cariole* until Monday?"

The clerk looked at the boy and smiled. "After coming all the way to Canada and rescuing Gabriel Tremblay, you deserve better treatment than this, don't you? If I can manage it, you shall have your *cariole* today."

"Great!" said Pete.

Henri told him the watchman lived not far from the freight station. "He has the key. Tell him that I said to let you into the warehouse to look for your *cariole*."

The man scribbled the watchman's address on a piece of paper and handed it to Pete. Excited, the boy ran out to the waiting sleigh and told the others the good news.

"Yikes! We're on the trail!" Ricky cried out as Pete climbed aboard.

"We'll get to the watchman's place in a jiffy," Marielle said as she sent the dappled horse on his way.

Five minutes later the duchess pulled up in front of a small wooden house on a side street. "I'd better speak to the watchman myself," she said, stepping down onto the street. "The chances are these people speak only French."

Marielle's knock on the door brought a quick response, but it was not from the watchman. Instead his wife answered and, after a brief conversation in French, she beckoned Marielle to step inside.

Two minutes went by, then three. The waiting children fidgeted, wondering what had happened.

"Maybe the watchman won't give up his key," Pete guessed.

"Or maybe he won't work on Saturday," was Pam's surmise.

"I hope Marielle comes out of there soon," Holly worried as she slapped her mittens together in order to warm her fingers.

Finally the door opened, and Marielle stepped out. She smiled at the woman and said, "*Merci, merci.*"

The duchess hopped into the sleigh and took up the reins. "You didn't bring the watchman," Ricky complained.

"He wasn't at home," Marielle said, and added that at first his wife had refused to give up a key to the warehouse. But after several minutes of persuasion, she had allowed Marielle to take a duplicate.

"I guess she let me take it because she recognized me as one of the duchesses," the young woman said, smiling.

"You're a beautiful, beautiful duchess!" Sue said as she wriggled more snugly onto Marielle's lap.

The warehouse was reached in a matter of a few more minutes. It was a gloomy-looking building, close to the freight depot. Marielle stopped the sleigh, and everyone quickly jumped out.

"Here's the main door," Pete said, pointing to a padlock which kept it locked.

Marielle took the key from her purse and inserted it in the lock, which popped open.

"Come on," Pete said. "Let's go inside."

"Where's the light switch?" Holly asked.

The children felt around on the wall but could not locate any switch.

"Well, we'll just have to be careful and not fall over anything," Marielle said as they stepped into the high-ceilinged warehouse.

"It's spooky inside here," Sue remarked.

"Don't be afraid," Pam said. "There's nothing to hurt——Eeek!"

Pam's sudden cry made everybody jump, and they immediately saw the cause of it. A mouse had scampered directly across their path and disappeared behind a stack of wooden crates.

The girl laughed at herself. "I'm not really afraid of mice. It was just that I was startled."

"You sure?" Ricky teased.

Boxes and other kinds of freight were piled here and there on the floor of the spacious building.

High above, the snow-covered skylights let in pale shafts of light.

"Do you suppose there are any bats in here?" Sue asked, clinging to Pam's hand as they walked along in their search for the *cariole*.

Finally Pete saw large double doors at one end of the building. "If our *cariole* is in here it will probably be near these doors," he said. "This is the only place where the sleigh could have been brought in."

But a search of the nearby area revealed nothing except more crates. One pile stood very high with three large boxes balanced one above the other.

"Here's one place we haven't looked yet," Ricky said.

"Where?" Pete asked.

"Behind these boxes."

"They're pretty heavy to move."

"I'll help you, Pete. We can both push together." The two boys put their shoulders to the bottom box.

"What are you doing?" Pam asked, hurrying over to them.

Pete gave an extra hard push. It caused the top crate to tilt far to one side. He did not realize this but Pam, looking up, exclaimed, "Look out!"

Her warning came just in time. The crate tipped farther and fell over just as the boys jumped out of the

"Look out!" Pam cried.

way. It crashed inches from where Ricky had stood.

"Oh!" Pam cried out in relief.

"Thanks, Sis," said Pete and Ricky together.

The three children lifted the box upright. Fortunately it had not been damaged in the fall.

"Now we can see what's behind here," Holly declared.

By standing on tiptoes she peered over the other boxes. But the *cariole* was not there!

"Oh, dear," said Marielle. "Do you suppose your sleigh has been stolen?"

"How could it be?" Pete said. "This place is always locked when the watchman is not here."

"Well," Marielle said, "let's return the key. I promised to bring it back immediately after the search."

Crestfallen, the children returned to the sleigh and rode back to the watchman's home. This time Ricky hopped out and knocked on the door. The woman opened it, and Marielle called to her from the sleigh, saying that they had not found the *cariole*.

"Perhaps we will see your husband on Monday," she called out in French.

Ricky got back into the sleigh, and they set off toward the hotel. This time, however, there was no gay chatter.

"Don't give up yet," Marielle said sympathetically. "I'll still help you in your search."

As she said this Marielle pulled on her left rein, and the horse turned a corner. Coming toward them was another *cariole* drawn by a white horse. Instantly the children were electrified by what they saw.

The cariole had the initials "H.H." *in gold letters on the front of it!*

"Our *cariole!* Stop!" Pete cried out to the driver. "Stop!"

The man kept straight ahead, paying no attention. Whether his beaver cap, pulled low over his ears, had prevented his hearing Pete or whether he had merely ignored the call, the Hollisters did not know. The driver continued on, urging his horse a little faster with a flick of the reins.

"Stop! Stop!" Pam begged. "You have our *cariole!*"

"Marielle, please turn around and catch him!" Holly burst out.

"Oh, dear, I must do something," the duchess said. "But the street is too narrow to turn here. I'll have to wait for the next crossing."

It was several hundred feet to the next cross street. By the time Marielle had turned her sleigh around and started off in pursuit, the *cariole* was far ahead but still in sight.

"Hurry, hurry, let's catch him!" Sue urged. She jiggled the reins in Marielle's hands, trying to make the dappled horse go faster. Finally the animal broke into a trot.

"Hurray, we're catching up!" Ricky cried out.

The driver of the *cariole* seemed oblivious of the pursuing children. He turned his head neither right nor left.

"That's strange," Pete whispered to Pam. "You'd think he'd try to duck down a side alley."

The rapid *clop, clop, clop* of the horses' hoofs in the hard-packed snow and the wind whistling in the children's faces added to the thrill of the chase. In a few minutes, they thought, they would have their very own *cariole*.

"We're gaining, we're gaining on him!" Ricky shouted as Marielle urged her horse even faster.

Just then, however, Pam groaned. "Look! The white is trotting too. That driver's trying to get away!"

CHAPTER 17

THE CANOE RACE

"FASTER! Faster!" Pete cried as the sleigh began to close the distance between the pursuing Hollisters and the fleeing *cariole.*

But at the next corner a large truck pulled across the intersection. The sleigh had to stop for a moment to allow the truck to go past.

"Yikes! What bad luck!" Ricky wailed. When the truck had moved along the Hollisters' sleigh was nowhere in sight.

"He must have turned down a side street," Marielle declared as she urged the horse on faster.

The Hollisters looked left and right at every street corner they came to, but their *cariole*, driven by the mysterious stranger, had made a clean getaway.

Marielle and the five children drove around the streets for an hour in a vain search. Then they drove to the police station and reported what had happened.

Sue took a nap after lunch, and Holly and Ricky spent a few hours tobogganing with Gram and Gramp.

During this time Pete, Pam, and Marielle again drove about the streets of the upper town and then the lower part of the city.

"It looks as if our *cariole* has vanished into thin air," Pete said finally.

"Maybe it's hidden in a garage somewhere," Pam guessed.

"Well, wherever it is," Marielle said in a hopeful tone, "your *cariole* is bound to appear on the streets again, and the police will spot it."

Shortly before suppertime the Quebec duchess deposited Pete and Pam at the hotel and drove off, saying she would get in touch with them the next day.

"And don't forget to watch the canoe race," she said as she waved good-by.

The next morning Gram said she could hardly realize that a week had gone by since they had set off on the trip from Shoreham to Quebec.

"So much has happened," Sue said with a giggle, "that it seems like a year, doesn't it?"

Church services over, the children began to feel the excitement which mounted hourly as the time for the big race approached. The sturdy river craft had gathered on the frozen surface of Princess Louise Basin, which was the starting point for the race. Gram and Gramp drove the children to the spot where they met the five Tremblay brothers and Victor.

"Are you all ready?" Sue asked.

"Yes, little one," Jean-Marc said, grinning.

Then Victor suggested, "Why don't we watch the race from the ferryboat?" He explained that the ferry took on hundreds of passengers and plied the St. Lawrence, well out of the way of the racing canoes.

"Let's do that," Pete said. "Then we can get a good view of the Tremblays during the entire race."

There was little time to lose because the ferry was ready to go shortly. Gramp drove the family and Victor down the hill to the lower city, where he parked the car. After buying the tickets they all trooped onto the ferryboat. It gave one toot and moved off amid the silently drifting ice floes of the big river. When it reached the middle, the ferryboat stopped and began to float gently downstream.

"Look over there," Victor said, pointing to Princess Louise Basin. "The race is just about to start."

The Hollisters could see nine canoes with their crews standing beside them ready for the starting gun. A shot echoed across the water. The racers pushed their canoes over the ice and launched them into the St. Lawrence. The race was on!

"Come on, come on, Tremblays!" Ricky shouted.

Now all the canoes were in the stream, and the rowers strained mightily as they paralleled the shore, racing upstream.

At Queen's Wharf, the boats angled across the river

The Tremblays pulled their boat over the ice.

toward the finish line on the Levis side. The crowd roared encouragement to one team, then another, as they rowed furiously through the open water between the ice floes.

"We're leading!" Pam cried out.

The Hollisters' friends had a slight edge as they dipped their oars with steady rhythm into the frigid water. But suddenly Victor groaned. A large ice floe, turning in the current, blocked the Tremblays' route.

"They're going to hit it!" Holly said. "Oh look!"

The canoe did hit the ice floe, but at that instant one of the brothers leaped out. He was followed by another who helped to pull the canoe onto the floe. Now all the Tremblays were on the ice, pushing and dragging their craft across it to the open water on the other side.

With a skill that was beautiful to behold they quickly launched the canoe again, hopping in at the same time. The Tremblays had dropped behind to second place, however, and were rowing furiously to catch up to the leader.

By this time the competing canoes were strung out in a line halfway across the river. One near the rear met bad luck when chunks of ice completely surrounded it and swept the craft downstream.

The Tremblays, meanwhile, battling for first place, gained slowly on the first boat. Then a chunk of ice blocked the leader momentarily. As it did, the Tremblay canoe, striving to reach a small open channel, made it just in time. The island rivermen were ahead by half a length.

"Go, go, go!" Pete shouted above the din of the other spectators crowding the rail of the ferryboat.

The Tremblays were the first to reach the ice jutting out from the Levis shore. Bent nearly double they pulled their boat over the final stretch.

Seeing his cousins' victory, Victor burst into a jolly French song and began to jig. "We did it! We did it!" he cried excitedly. "We could not have won without the Happy Hollisters."

The onlookers watched as one canoe then another reached the finish line. After that the ferry pulled into the dock at Levis. The band was playing gaily. A mighty cheer went up as the victors made their way up the gangplank and onto the ferry for the return trip.

It was almost ten minutes before the Tremblay brothers could break away from the backslapping and handshaking of the enthusiastic crowd and reach the spot where the Hollisters were waiting for them.

"We're so proud of you!" Pam said as they all congratulated the victorious rivermen.

"We couldn't disappoint our little friends," Jean-Marc said with a grin. He picked Sue up and carried her on his shoulders to the upper deck while the others followed.

On the way back across the river toward Quebec, Pete told the Tremblays in detail of the chase the day before.

"We nearly had our *cariole* but we lost it at the last minute," Pete said.

"Did you get a look at the man driving?" asked Victor.

"I did," said Holly.

"Would you recognize him again if you saw him?" Victor continued.

"Oh yes."

The ferryboat edged its way through the thickening floes until it was a hundred yards from the Quebec side of the river. Holly, who had been scanning the passengers crowded on the deck below, suddenly screamed, "I see him, I see him!"

She pointed to a man who was shouldering his way through the crowd in order to be one of the first off the gangplank.

"There's the man who stole our *cariole!*" Holly cried out again.

"Come on," Pete said, "let's get him!"

But descending the stairs through the milling crowd was not easy. By the time the Hollisters reached the lower deck the ferryboat had touched the wharf, and the gangplank was in place.

"Hurry, hurry!" Holly wailed. "We must get him."

Despite their efforts, however, the man squeezed onto the gangplank ahead of them and hurried ashore.

"Don't worry," Victor said. "He won't get away from us."

Pete was close on the heels of the Tremblays when they reached the street outside the ferry terminal.

"There he goes!" the boy cried.

The man was walking in a leisurely manner along the street.

"Stop, stop!" Pete cried out, and Paul Tremblay added, "*Arrêtez-vous, arrêtez-vous!*"

Hearing this, the fellow looked around. Pete grabbed one of his arms and Paul the other.

A surprised look came over their prisoner's face. "What do you want?" he asked in French.

The Tremblays quickly told him of their suspicions.

"But I am not a thief!" the man protested.

"Then why did you have the Hollisters' *cariole?*" Victor demanded.

The children looked on expectantly as the French words flashed back and forth.

"Oh!" Victor said finally. "That explains it."

He told the children that their prisoner was the watchman at the freight office. The fellow had admired the *cariole* and had merely been trying it out the day before.

"Where is it now?" Pete asked.

"In the warehouse garage. We will go there immediately."

As the building was not far away, they all went on foot. The watchman produced the key and opened the door. There stood the *cariole*.

Shouts of joy filled the air as the children hastened forward to touch the beautiful sleigh.

"You like it, eh?" Victor Tremblay asked, knowing full well what the answer would be.

"We love it! We love it!" Pam said.

"You did a beautiful job, Victor!" Pete cried.

The five children scrambled into the *cariole* as their grandparents and the Tremblays looked on, smiling approval.

The watchman spoke effusively again, and when Victor translated he said, "He wants to make it up to you by hiring a horse so you can ride in your *cariole* today."

The watchman hastened off and returned five minutes later, leading a small white horse which he hitched to the *cariole*.

"Do you think you can drive it alone, Pete?" Victor Tremblay asked.

"I'm sure I can," Pete replied. The boy had often driven Domingo and felt able to manage the sleigh, even though it was crowded with passengers.

"We will have to go now," Victor said, "to visit relatives in town."

"See you later, alligator," Ricky called as the men left.

Gram and Gramp turned back to the dock to pick up their parked car, saying that they would meet the children at the hotel.

"Giddap, giddap," Pete said, and the horse pulled the *cariole* out into the narrow streets of the lower town.

"Hurray, we've got it!" Ricky called out. "Won't Mother and Daddy be glad?"

As Pete guided the horse to the top of the steep hill, he made a left-hand turn. But he executed this too sharply. The left runner of the *cariole* went high on a snowbank and the sleigh tilted dangerously.

"Hang on!" Pam cried out.

But the sudden jolt caught everyone off guard. The Happy Hollisters were thrown out onto the snow-filled street.

CHAPTER 18

ALOUETTE, ALOUETTE

IN A scramble of arms and legs the youngsters tumbled out of the *cariole* and landed in the street. Pete and Pam were the first to pick themselves up. Sheepishly they helped Ricky and Holly and Sue to their feet. The little dark-haired girl was crying bitterly.

"Oh, dear," Pam said as she brushed the snow from Sue's coat. "Where are you hurt, honey?"

"I'm not hurt," Sue replied, the tears streaming down her cheeks.

"Then why are you crying?" Pete asked.

"Our nice new *cariole* is broken."

"No, it isn't!" Ricky said. "Look!"

The horse had gone a few paces, then stopped, bringing the sleigh to a halt on level ground.

Seeing this, Sue decided to laugh.

"You look funny laughing with tears in your eyes," Holly told her.

"I thought our nice new sleigh got lopsided all at once," Sue explained. "But I'm glad to see it isn't."

None of her brothers and sisters had received anything worse than a shaking up in the fall. Now they piled back into the sleigh. Pete took the reins, and soon they were at the hotel. Holly was the first inside the door.

"Mommy! Daddy!" she cried as she saw Mr. and Mrs. Hollister standing at the desk in the lobby.

The four others rushed in behind her to greet their parents.

"We're so glad to see you!"

"The mystery is solved!"

"We found the *cariole!*"

"And rescued Gabriel!"

When the children had calmed down a little, Pam asked, "Has Domingo been found?"

"Yes!" Mrs. Hollister replied, beaming.

"Tell us all about it!" Pete urged.

Just then Gram and Gramp stepped off the elevator and hastened to greet the newcomers. Then, as all listened quietly, Mrs. Hollister explained that two migrant workers, living in a shack in the woods near Shoreham, had taken Domingo.

"You mean they stole him?" Pete asked with a surprised look.

"Not exactly," Mrs. Hollister replied. She said that Officer Cal, who had finally located the burro, had questioned the two men. It seemed that Joey and Will had told the pair that the Hollisters wanted the two men to take care of Domingo while the family was on a trip. Seeing a chance to make money by giving burro rides to children, the pair had come and taken the donkey away.

"Then Joey and Will were at the bottom of it after all," Pam declared, exasperated.

"Well, the boys apologized to us," Mr. Hollister said, "and Domingo is back safe in his stall."

They all entered the elevator and went to the Hollisters' suite, where the youngsters regaled their parents with tales of the exciting week in Canada.

"The final parade is tomorrow night," Pete said. "May we stay to see it, Mother?"

It was agreed that they would remain for the crowning event of the Winter Carnival.

The rest of that Sunday and most of the next day were spent sight-seeing. It was not until late in the afternoon that Marielle called at the hotel. The children excitedly told her about the finding of the *cariole*.

"Oh, I'm so glad!" she said, then added, "I have a big secret to tell you."

"Are we going to have another adventure?" Ricky asked.

"You can call it that," Marielle said, smiling. "How would you all like to ride on a float tonight?"

"In the big parade?" Pam asked.

Marielle said "Yes." Several members of the parade committee, having seen the Hollister children in costume at the Coliseum, had invited them to ride on the float of *Alouette*.

"Great!" Pete said. "But I thought that *Alouette* was a French song."

The duchess said indeed it was. The floats that evening all were to depict French-Canadian songs. She told them that *Alouette*, the skylark, would be a giant figure on the float. "But I'm afraid the poor bird has only a few feathers left," she said, "because it was plucked."

Hearing this, Gram Hollister laughed and began to sing:

> "*Alouette, gentille alouette,*
> *Alouette, je t'y plumerai.*"

"That's it!" Marielle said, beaming. "You know the words. Well, you can sing the song tonight as the float goes by."

After supper the Hollisters donned warm clothes under their costumes. Marielle called for them and showed the children the long line of floats and the people on them.

At the end of the line was a float on which the queen was seated in a coach. It looked like a huge tiara. The queen wore an ermine wrap and a white crown and carried a scepter.

"Oh, isn't she beautiful?" Pam exclaimed.

The Hollisters now went to take their places on

Ricky plucked a plume from Alouette.

one of the floats. Soon the parade started, with bands playing, clowns dancing, and chubby *Bonhommes Carnavals* prancing back and forth on the line of march. Torchlights carried by the paraders lighted up the streets, giving a fairyland effect to the jolly scene. The sidewalks were lined with thousands of happy, singing townspeople.

The elder Hollisters stood at the side of the hotel while the parade passed. How they enjoyed the float showing "*Sur le Pont d'Avignon!*" The bridge was lighted up, and dancers swayed to and fro on it. Next came "*Bonbons, Caramels, Chocolat.*" This float showed a big Eskimo eating candies and ice-cream bars.

Gram and Mrs. Hollister clapped gaily when the next float came along. Everybody burst out singing, "*Marie-Anne s'en va-t-au Moulin,*"—"Mary Ann is going to the mill." The float showed a big windmill, with Mary Ann and her donkey, and a wolf watching nearby.

Following this came "*La Cane du Canada,*" the duck of Canada. On the high float was a giant duck and smaller ones playing musical instruments and singing. Next, came a display which made the onlookers howl with laughter. A tremendous green cabbage lay in a garden, with worms poking their heads out of it. It depicted the song "*Savez-vous planter des choux?"* meaning "Do you know how to plant cabbages?"

Now another band followed, and behind it came the *Alouette* float. Instantly the crowd burst into song. The big skylark with but a few plumes left in his tail looked as if he might be freezing. Pete, Pam, Holly, Ricky, and Sue bowed and waved to the crowd. As the float passed the elder Hollisters, Ricky impishly plucked one of the few remaining plumes from the tail of poor *Alouette,* and the crowd cheered wildly.

"Isn't this the most marvelous parade ever?" Pam whispered to Pete as they glanced behind them.

Following was the line of duchesses in beautiful horse-drawn carriages. Pam waved to Marielle, the first in line. Marielle waved back and threw a kiss.

One after another the duchesses passed. Last was the queen herself. She smiled and nodded as the crowd pressed closer to get a better look at the Quebec beauty.

The parade ended with everyone singing the catchy carnival song:

> "*Carnaval, Mardi Gras, Carnaval*
> *A Quebec c'est tout un festival.*
> *Carnaval, Mardi Gras, Carnaval*
> *Chantons tous le joyeux Carnaval.*"

As the Happy Hollister children climbed down from the float, they were met by six husky, cheering men,

Victor Tremblay and his five cousins. Each of the rivermen swung one of the Hollisters up to his broad shoulders. As they tramped back toward the hotel the jolly rivermen burst out with "*Alouette, Alouette*" and the crowd answered "*Je t'y plumerai.*"